# HOTEL HIGHWAY

## Very Most Famous

By Sudha Challa

Disclaimer

This is purely a work of fiction. The names, characters, places and events depicted in this story are all products of the author's imagination. Any similarities to real people or places are purely coincidental.

No part of this work may be reproduced or stored or transmitted in any form or by any means without the specific and written permission of the author/publisher.

# Dedication

This book is dedicated to the memory of my parents, Lalitha and Radhakrishnamurthy Challa.

I am forever indebted to them for their love, guidance, generosity, the values they instilled in me and for encouraging me to get an education and to follow my dreams.

# Acknowledgements

This book would not have been possible but for my dear friends, Sudha Dara, Surendra Dara and Kalyani, who spent a good deal of their precious time reading the manuscript and gave me invaluable guidance, encouragement and support. This book would not exist without the support, brilliant insight, changes and suggestions of my amazing editor, Pranav Dixit, who helped steer the ship towards the shores of clarity and perspicacity.

# Contents

Radha.................................................................................. 1

Kamalnath and the Restaurant ................................. 45

Shanta ..................................................................... 80

Dhananjay................................................................ 86

# Hotel Highway – Very Most Famous

*Better than a foolish son
Is one deceased or never born
The pain given at least is brief
But the fool is cause for lifelong grief
(From the Panchatantra)*

## Radha

How does a couple start a conversation after not having seen or spoken to each other for over sixteen years? Radha wondered. She was in the car on her way to meet Prabhakar, her husband. Checking her watch, fidgeting with her clothes, running her hand over her hair and tucking an unruly curl behind her ear, she wondered if they would be able to recognise each other. Time, inexorable in its pursuit of eternity, dealt with everything: living, breathing and pulsing, stationary and inanimate in its own way. With some, time was kind; with others, time was punishing, and she was afraid that time may not have been that kind to her. While getting ready, she had changed her attire three times.

The first saree she tried on was a solid grey colour with rich texture, a golden border embossed with dancing figures oozing solemnity and dignity, giving the sense of being grounded. Not a bad choice for the occasion. She did not like it, though, thinking that it made her look old and tired. Then, she picked up a colourful saree with diagonal lines, small pink roses and a wide green border, a saree that the children had gone with Mamayya, her father-in-law, to buy for her for one Diwali, four years ago. It was many years since she had gone shopping for clothes, not even for festive occasions. Yes, she had gone to buy her children's uniforms, an annual ritual, as long as they were in school. Her two sons, Vasu and Mukund and her daughter Sunanda, all grown up now, eager to make their own decisions and confident of their choices, went shopping instead. Every year before Diwali, the three of them went to the city to buy clothes for themselves, their mother and their grandfather. Radha cherished the fact that the three siblings got along so well and that the two boys doted upon their sister, she being the youngest and the most domineering when it came to choosing clothes. Sometimes they would ask her to accompany them, but more often than not, she would decline. This afternoon, she found the second saree too festive and discarded that. Finally, she selected the saree she really liked, a pale-yellow silk with small embroidered motifs in white. It was a gift from Prabhakar's sister, Parvati, for one of the festivals. She could not remember which. Parvathi was older than Prabhakar and worked as a teacher in the local government school. She showed good taste in almost everything, and her selection of clothes was excellent and more to Radha's liking, tending towards the lighter and pastel shades. Parvati's husband, Arun, was an administrator in the local electricity board and was going to be retiring very soon. Parvati was a good seamstress during her spare time and even stitched the blouse for this particular saree she gifted to Radha. The blouse was of a matching colour with a yellow body, a wide white border at the back and long sleeves. The saree and blouse ensemble appeared subdued, thought Radha, and in a way complemented her personality. She decided she was going to wear something that she really liked and perhaps gain some confidence from it. She was not up to date with the fashions; she never had been, her clothes and the way she wore her hair always being practical and functional. Sunanda, her daughter, with the vivacity, hubris and ebullience of youth, armed with the knowledge of the latest fashions, pundit of recent hairstyles and cosmetics, would sometimes choose the clothes for her mother when they went out together, a rarity. On those occasions, Sunanda would also try to convince Radha to wear her hair differently to keep up with the latest trends. Radha had checked herself in the mirror one last time before she came out of her room. She let out a long, deep sigh, resigned to her appearance. Her neck was bare, and she was tempted to wear a necklace that matched the saree. She took out the necklace from the top drawer of the dresser and placed it against herself. It was a delicate piece of handicraft with small rhinestones from which fine yellow and white beads hung, lace-like, helping to cover the area above the blouse, lending an exquisite elegance. She sighed again, replacing the necklace in its box. The last thing she wanted was for Prabhakar to think that she dressed up for him. If anyone had told her that she was a handsome woman, not someone you called pretty, they would not have been wrong. She was perhaps well put together, of medium complexion, with an imperfect nose, the bridge slightly curved, slanting eyes (an inheritance apparently from her father's sister), generous lips, a round chin and high cheek bones which seemed to dominate her face, giving the sense of stability and dependability. She wanted to be assured and firm and wanted to face Prabhakar without trepidation. She still had not made up her mind as to what she would say or what her decision would be. As she walked out of the house, she wondered where everyone was. Mamayya, saying he had an errand to run, had taken off an hour earlier. The children were nowhere to be seen. It was odd, she thought, that they had left her alone at this crucial juncture after all the cautionary comments and injunctions they had showered her with during the past many weeks. She was tempted to call each one of them to find out where they were. Yes, it was a week day, but Sunanda had a few days off before her term exams and yet was not in her room. Earlier, Mukund, her second son, said he was working from the home office preparing some legal documents, but when she peered inside his office, he was not there, and Vasu who had three days off, a respite after doing night shift at the medical centre for a whole month, a crucial part of his internship, was nowhere to be found. She so desperately wished that at least one of them had been there to see her off as she left for this stress-provoking and potentially life-changing rendezvous. Sixteen years ago, she was devastated when Prabhakar deserted them, her confidence in herself being irrevocably shaken, and any faith that she had in herself as a wife and a companion was dealt a severe blow. Prabhakar had been a handsome man. She had always been conscious that when they were together, they were not matched in looks and that he was the better looking of the two. Did he metamorphose well? She was thankful that her three children had inherited their good looks from Prabhakar and his side of the family and not from her.

Tony, her assistant, had been waiting by the van. He saw to it that Radha was properly seated before getting behind the wheel. On any other day, Radha would have sat at the front, next to Tony. But this afternoon, she felt she wanted the spaciousness of the back seat to clear and calm her mind. As Tony started the engine and eased off the brake, the van glided on the gravel path leading from the house to the small road, which then connected to the highway, the crunching sound of the gravel unusually loud. They had been planning to cement the driveway for several years, but something or the other had come up every time, mostly to do with the business of the nursery. The tall elephant ear crotons on either side of the driveway were symmetrical, their large brilliant green leaves spread out as though calling out to the sun. The leaves were large enough to wrap an infant in, Radha thought. Her experienced gardener's eyes took in the shorter caladiums skirting the elephant ear crotons, their leaves with the green fringes encircling the darker red and maroon centres with red and green lines radiating outward, small white dots scattered across them like wash paintings or small artist's palettes. The plumeria trees with the flowers, white and yellow and red, stood inside the border of the crotons, their inflorescences raised to the skies as though in silent prayer, prompting Radha to join her own hands in a quick gesture to the powers that be. She was not sure how her meeting with Prabhakar would go and what the outcome was going to be. The restaurant with its adjacent temple they were heading to was halfway between their township and the city, and on a good day without much traffic on the highway, it took about an hour to get there. When they moved into their new house about eight years ago, it was considered to be on the outskirts of their large town, with only two wine shops in the neighbourhood and very little else. She along with Mamayya chose this site after much deliberation, because it was cheaper and affordable and there was a three-fourths acre of vacant space for the nursery behind the house. Within eight years though, the town expanded and grew around the house and the nursery, and now they were more near the centre than at the perimeter of the town. The wine shops had long since closed, being replaced by other business enterprises, and a large mall was being constructed about a mile from the house and the nursery.

She wanted to be at the restaurant more than an hour ahead of the appointed time so that she could collect her thoughts and be ready for her encounter with Prabhakar. In a few minutes, they reached the highway and were cruising towards their destination. Radha felt far from being presentable and was dreading meeting Prabhakar. The strong force of his nature—the very signature of Prabhakar, his domineering presence, his singular lack of sensitivity for the feelings of others, especially hers, and his ability to demolish any opposition—suddenly loomed in front of her like a wall she would be unable to scale. The memory of his characteristics and habits, which she had forgotten over the years, now resurfaced. The many times (too many times) he had belittled her, snubbed her or merely ignored her or her suggestions came back to cause ripples in her confidence. She had always been a little meek by nature, afraid to be adventurous, reticent, with a tendency to give in easily to others' demands, something that Prabhakar exploited completely. The memory of his constant unvoiced disapproval of her now reared its head like an unpleasant spectre. Her heart was racing in spite of her many attempts to calm it down. She had rehearsed snippets of her imaginary conversation with Prabhakar a dozen times since she spoke to him a little over twenty-four hours ago. Strangely, he did not ask to speak to his father, and Radha wondered if it was out of fear of what Mamayya may say.

"Where are the children?" Prabhakar would ask as the scene played out in her head.

"They were busy this evening," she would say, or, if she wanted to be hostile and proud, "They were not interested in meeting you." Merely thinking of this second response gave her a strange satisfaction, but she was also annoyed at this pent-up hostility within her. Somewhere during the long arduous sixteen years since his sudden departure, Radha had managed to school herself to accept the desertion by Prabhakar and to throw the waters of forgiveness on the burning embers of resentment against him. She never had the opportunity of examining her relationship with him for the ten years that they had shared. The minutiae of their married life seemed to have somehow escaped her notice; she had been so busy with the arrival of the children and taking care of the household as well as Atthayya, her mother in-law, who was ill. Atthayya had a liver condition, unremitting in its progress, not amenable to any particular treatment, this diagnosis being first given at the local clinic and later at a large hospital in the city. Radha had hoped that with proper care, her mother in law's condition would improve, but over the course of five years, Atthayya became bed ridden, and taking care of her every need as well as the needs of her children had kept her busy. On some days, it seemed that Atthayya was not even aware of her surroundings. It was at this stage that Prabhakar had left. Radha often wondered during the first few months of

Prabhakar's absence if his mother's incurable illness had driven him away, for she knew that some people were incapable of handling so many responsibilities.

During the ten years that they shared together, she was never able to express her displeasure regarding Prabhakar's behaviour towards her; even if she had, he would probably have brushed it aside calling it her imagination, such had been his nature. She realized that she had always been a little intimidated by him. Now, as she sat in the car, her palms were damp with perspiration, the butterflies in her stomach doing a merry go round, her mouth was dry and she felt that she could not swallow. It suddenly dawned upon her that she had not eaten since morning, caught up as she had been, in the work at the nursery and getting ready for this meeting. She had a panic attack and suddenly felt nauseated as she realized that she may not have the wherewithal of confronting Prabhakar or resisting any demands he made. Lowering the car window, she tried to get some fresh air into her lungs, but the feeling of being choked stayed with her. Abruptly, she asked Tony to stop. Tony pulled the van over to the side of the road and stopped under a large neem tree. Radha stumbled out and took several deep breaths. This was a bad idea, she thought, and wanted to turn back and return to the nursery, which had become her second home, her refuge and the source of her strength and confidence, where she still had so many unfinished tasks.

The nursery, with its damp coolness, the wet earth, the many mingled smells of the plants with their different blooms, made her forget the rest of the world. The orderliness in her nursery—with the plants arranged in tiers, larger ones at the bottom, smaller ones at the top, with the fruit and vegetable plants in a separate section—was in contradistinction to the chaos now reigning in her head and her heart. On any given day, she spent at least ten hours in the nursery taking care of her plants and working alongside the two gardeners she had employed once the business had become profitable. At the beginning, she worked alone, fourteen to sixteen hours, digging, planting and potting, getting the plants ready to be shipped to her different customers. Around their house both old and new, she had grown her own personal garden and had cultivated roses, lilies, sunflowers, marigolds, jasmines and multihued crotons, to name but a few. At the back of the house, she had grown tomatoes, lemons, oranges, banana, plantain, papaya and mango trees, the very same plants also being cultivated in her large nursery.

Tony got out of the driver's seat and came rushing to her side. She put out her hand and placed it on the tree for support, her back bent, as she took in deep breaths. The tree was large with a straight wide trunk, its girth reflecting its age, its branches reaching upwards and outwards like arms eager to spread their shade, quintessential Mother Nature, with her unquestioned generosity. As she leant against the tree, she chided herself for not having listened to Mamayya's advice of simply ignoring Prabhakar's letter.

Prabhakar's first letter arrived three months ago in a thick envelope addressed to her with their old address on it, brought to their doorstep by the postmaster, Mr. Das, himself. He was a good friend of Mamayya's and was very excited. "It is a letter from America. I thought I would bring it over on my way home." Mr. Das's son Murali, and Prabhakar had been high school classmates and Mr. Das was well acquainted with what Prabhakar had done. Radha could recall distinctly the time and the day that the letter had arrived. An unexpected rain had merely dampened the earth on that day, the wet ground releasing its characteristic petrichor, reminding one of the hot summer months yet to come. "This fragrance that the earth emits when dampened by the first rain is from plant oils and chemicals from bacteria released from the earth," Mukund, her younger son who had learnt about it in his science class, had once told her.

She invited Mr. Das in, and after he was comfortably ensconced in one of the cushioned chairs, Radha looked at the sender's address. When she saw Prabhakar's name, her heart skipped a beat. At the very bottom, she read the words "Chicago, Illinois, USA." Leaving Mamayya and Mr. Das chatting about all the sundry topics including the local politics, the weather, the state of the post office and what Mr. Das was planning after his impending retirement, Radha had gone in quickly to get some tea and snacks for both of them. It was another hour before Mr. Das left. As he was leaving, appreciative of the hospitality, Mr. Das said, "Radha, open the letter and read it. Maybe there is some good news."

Radha had smiled and said, "That is good news sixteen years too late, Mr. Das," whereupon he laughed, waved a good bye and left on his motorcycle.

The envelope was heavy. She gave it to Mamayya. He held the envelope for a long time, turned it this way and that as though divining its contents from its weight like a mystic, and just when she thought he was going to open it, he had handed it back to her saying, "It is for you, Radha. Open it." She had always appreciated the fact that Mamayya had treated her with respect despite her situation and desperation and during the worst of times. There had been no difference in the love and affection he had shown his own children and her. She was thankful that her hands were steady as she used the sandalwood letter opener and slit through the envelope. The letter opener was long, slender and elegant with a beautiful carving on the handle, reminding one of royalty and princes, palaces and grandeur. Mr. Gopal, an old friend of the family who had been on a trip to Mysore, had brought this as a gift and had told them, "It is made from sandalwood from which the oil has not been extracted. When the oil is extracted from the wood, the wood does not retain its fragrance for long." Along with the letter opener, he had given them a framed picture of the Mysore Maharajah's palace. That was two years after Prabhakar had left. Radha still remembered the sudden longing she experienced to travel to Mysore and visit the beautiful palace._The farthest she had travelled in her life was to the city across the mountains. Just as she took in the smell of the sandalwood in a long deep breath, the thick wad of papers from the envelope spilled onto the ground. Prabhakar was finally filing for a divorce, she thought at that time, and then immediately wondered why he had waited all these years. It was strange that the thought of filing for a divorce from Prabhakar had never occurred to her during all these years. She had been brought up with the firm belief that when you married, you were married for life, and she had believed that her life with Prabhakar would be forever. The papers were cream coloured with a serrated red border, with Prabhakar's writing on them. There were no typewritten words to indicate that it was a legal document.

Sixteen years ago, after his abrupt departure, she ardently waited for days on end for a word from him. A letter, even a one sentence letter, to let them know about his whereabouts, to let them know that they, herself, the children, still mattered in his life, would have been eagerly accepted by her. But there was no letter. Nor was there any phone call. She developed an ague. Her temperature was up as though her heated brain, with its dire thoughts and ideas, had invaded her whole body. She did not eat for three days, nor did she feel any thirst. She lay there upon the creaky cot, resting on the thick interwoven ropes, allowing the rough-hewn ropes to bite into the bare skin exposed on her back between the blouse and the saree she wore. She would get up only when necessary, not talking to anyone, ignoring the children and their wants, her in-laws, the whole world. Her hair became matted. The knots in her hair represented the knots in her mind, her mind frozen in time and space. Her muscles ached with her internal pain. She, who had been so diligent about Atthayya's care, neglected even that. The suddenness and deliberate coldness of Prabhakar's departure had shocked her. Mamayya hid his rage under a camouflage of the preoccupation with the daily routine, waking the two older boys and getting them ready for school, rushing to his garment store to open it for his employees and running the necessary errands essential for the household. She was oblivious to the fact that Mamayya, in his own fumbling way, was cooking for the children and Atthayya and that he had taken upon himself the mantel of her multifarious tasks. Finally, it was Mamayya who cajoled her, made her get up and start her routine again.

"What will happen to the children if you behave like this?" In the ten years that she had known him, he had never admonished her for anything. She heard the recrimination in his voice now. She had to make a choice. Either she chose life and sustenance or she chose inactivity and a vegetative state. For three days, she walked barefoot, willing the stones and debris around the yard to bite into her soles, letting the stimulus of pain penetrate into her consciousness, freeing her from the anesthesia of a shocked mind and soul. She even worried about going mad. Madness was an entity she had never understood. It happened to other people, people like Shanta, the somewhat dishevelled woman who lived on the other side of the Hanuman Mountain. Local rumor had it that Shanta had three miscarriages. Her husband had abandoned her. Despondency, social ostracism, had driven her to madness—or so everyone said. About two years before Prabhakar left, they had gone to the Hanuman temple on Mamayya's birthday. Mamayya_was an ardent devotee of Lord Hanuman and religiously made offerings to this God at the temple on his birthday and other important days. Lying on her cot, Radha recalled what a beautiful day it had been and how, for the first time since she had married Prabhakar, they had all gone out together as a family. Suresh, Prabhakar's younger brother and a policeman who worked in the city, his wife, Nirmala, Parvathi and her husband were also with them, with their children. Atthayya, who could not climb up the steps to the temple, had stayed at home. The adults trailed behind while the older children, all excited, climbed up the steps, agile and nimble, looking in awe at the spread of the valley around them, pointing out to each other the distant mountains and the chain of cars and lorries on the highway, intermittently looking longingly and pointing at the colourful balloons and the multihued cotton candy sold by the hawkers around the temple. Sunanda, who was two years old and just then learning to be independent, wanted to climb up the steps on her own. Radha had held Sunanda's hand as she put one faltering step after another and wondered at what point she was going to get tired and would demand to be carried. She had expected Prabhakar to hold Sunanda's other hand and lead her up, but he did nothing of the kind. Instead, his entire demeanor had been one of impatience and irritation. At that point, Shanta appeared on the steps ahead, blocking their path. On Shanta's outstretched hand, there were several candies, red, orange and green. Shanta looked beautiful even with her uncombed hair and her crumpled blouse and saree. This was the first time Radha had come face to face with Shanta and she was wondering what to do when Sunanda extended her tiny hand to take one of the proffered candies. Suddenly, Prabhakar came in between Sunanda and Shanta and rudely pushed Shanta's hand away, making the candies scatter upon the steps, yelling at her and calling her a mad woman who had no right to be there harassing everyone, and asking her to get out of his sight. The friendly, guileless smile on Shanta's face was extinguished like a small lamp in the ferocity of an angry wind. She left with an indecipherable look on her face. Radha had wanted to apologise to Shanta for Prabhakar's behavior but did not get the chance.

Radha, overcome with guilt and shame at the way her husband had behaved towards a helpless woman, said, "You shouldn't have pushed her hand away or shouted that way at Shanta," whereupon Prabhakar had said without any remorse, "Stop taking her side. So, you even know her name?"

"Yes, her father was one of the temple's senior priests who has recently retired. Didn't you know that?"

"What does it matter whether he was the senior temple priest or the temple sweeper. This mad woman was abandoned by her husband and she is here making a nuisance of herself, troubling and frightening all the visitors," Prabhakar said and then took off, leaving her and Sunanda trailing behind._

Sixteen years ago, in the aftermath of Prabhakar's departure, it dawned on Radha, what it felt to be abandoned by the very person you had trusted, the very person who was supposed to be there for you through the good times and the bad. Now, years later, Shanta had become a good friend, always following Radha around when she went to the restaurant to run her errands.

On the seventh day after Prabhakar had left, Mamayya handed her a small stainless tumbler of coffee and spoke to her hesitantly, "Radha, there is something I have to tell you." It was late afternoon, the boys had not yet returned from school, Sunanda was taking her afternoon nap, and Radha was getting ready to prepare dinner so that she could first feed Athhayya, who was confined almost completely to her bed by now. It was Mamayya's hesitation that caught her attention. Mamayya had always exuded strength and confidence, a confidence borne out of the fact that, despite his own humble beginnings, his three children had come up in life and done well for themselves. Of the three, he had been particularly proud of Prabhakar's achievements. Prabhakar, the eldest, was a professor in business management in a local college and had come up in the ranks by dint of his hard work and knowledge and had earned a good reputation as a teacher. This afternoon, though, Mamayya was looking at her over the frame of his glasses as he said these words, his demeanor apologetic, his head bent in supplication or shame. His eyes anxiously clambered over the brown plastic frames of his glasses as though looking at her through the transparency of the lenses would somehow deprive his words of their gravity and steal his words of their veracity. She raised the glass of coffee to her lips, sipping from it, her eyes fixed upon Mamayya. "There is something I want you to know…" he mumbled, not as clearly as before. She felt like a little sparrow, waiting for the shaft of lightning to strike, helpless, shivering in the unexpected storm, with the primal knowledge of the inevitability of things. If only Lord Hanuman, with his divine superhuman strength and courage, could step in the way of that bolt of lightning, catch it and annihilate it, as only he knew how—then, that sparrow would be spared. But it was not to be. Mamayya's voice was trembling with emotion as he said, "I have a friend. His son is a mechanic at the airport. He said that he saw Prabhakar with a woman, boarding a plane to London."

She felt a sudden pain tear through her chest, and a chill enveloped her as she heard the mention of this other woman. She wrapped her palms around the steel container with the hot coffee, allowing the heat to sear through the skin and numb the internal pain that was choking her. Radha was always surprised at how the knowledge of the other woman with whom Prabhakar left for London caused this unbearable feeling of being deceived, even after many years—that feeling of being betrayed, after what she thought was a decent, stable marriage, after three children. Her expectations of Prabhakar had been few, but one of them had been of his loyalty and faithfulness as a husband. She looked at Mamayya as he narrated the role of this woman, Leena, in Prabhakar's life. Leena was from a wealthy business family and had been junior to Prabhakar in college, where they had met and fallen in love. When they wanted to marry, there had been objections from both their families. Atthayya had gone on a hunger strike, shunning food and refusing to speak for an entire week. The blistering disapproval from both his parents had stalled

Prabhakar. He did not mention Leena again, and there had been an uneasy truce at home. Mamayya related that Prabhakar, who had always been very close to his mother, became very distant with her, holding her responsible for his separation from Leena. His relationship with his mother became rather tenuous, his conversations with her becoming monosyllabic; things never went back to being normal between mother and son, even after Prabhakar's wedding.

While Mamayya related this story, Radha realized that she had become the Leena alternative, a poor substitute, perhaps. In a subtle but pervasive manner, Leena became the yardstick of comparison for Radha. In her mind's eye, all Radha could envision was someone beautiful, glamorous and far more intelligent and accomplished than herself, a comparison that subdued any anger against Prabhakar, a comparison which in the ensuing months gradually chiselled away at her confidence as a woman, mother and wife. At that moment, when she learnt about Leena, she wanted to ask Mamayya if he had any photographs of her and had quelled that question, thinking it was not appropriate and that her curiosity about Leena may be somehow deemed absurd, childish or even petty. Radha, however, could not subdue her own inner turmoil, curiosity and questions about Leena and had gone to the large cupboard in their bedroom where Prabhakar kept his clothes and other belongings, including his checkbook and bank documents. She, who had always respected Prabhakar's privacy, was now galvanized by a desperate search for the truth about Leena as she pulled out the drawers and searched beneath his folded clothes and inside the pockets of the trousers and jackets he had left hanging behind, for any pictures of Leena, any proof of her presence in Prabhakar's life. She found none.

As she was shutting the topmost drawer, her eyes fell upon what appeared to be a piece of wood. It was hiding under a sheaf of papers, which had hastily scribbled notes Prabhakar had made for one of his lectures in the college. Her heart beating forcefully against her chest, she had pulled out that piece of wood. It was a decorative plaque, broken in half, with a sculpted border, the type of plaque one could hang on the wall or display on one's desk, with Prabhakar's name across it in beautiful calligraphy. She then realized that the other half must have had Leena's name on it. For many years, Leena became an invisible presence, a wound upon her psyche and Prabhakar's abandonment of her and the children, a blister upon her soul; the fractured wooden plaque had turned into a symbol and testament of Prabhakar and Leena's undying love for one another.

Sixteen years ago, when Suresh with his wife, Nirmala, and Parvathi with her husband rushed to their house as soon as they got the news of the absconding Prabhakar, they spoke in whispers, afraid that the children would hear and be traumatized. Suresh was angry with Mamayya for not giving him the news sooner.

"I could have stopped him, I could have reasoned with him," Suresh had said, grinding his teeth, his fists balled up.

An equally angry Mamayya had asked, "He did not even say goodbye to me. He sneaked out like a coward. Even if he had told me, how could I have reasoned with a foolish man and a donkey? He left without saying much to Radha, no mention of his destination or when he would return. He only told her that he was leaving the country. I thought he would return soon. It was only three days later, when I ran into Parthasarathy, my bank friend, that I learnt Prabhakar had closed his bank account. That is when the realization hit us that he had left for good. A week later I learnt from a colleague of Prabhakar whom I ran across in the market, that he had resigned from his job in the college. Did I not have the right to know that? Didn't Radha as his wife have the right to know that?"

"He closed his bank account and he resigned from his job without informing either of you?" Suresh was incredulous. "Did he leave any money for Radha or the children or for you?" Suresh was identical to Prabhakar in looks but with a slightly smaller frame. In demeanor and character, Prabhakar and Suresh were poles apart. While Suresh always had a sympathetic ear for other's troubles, ready to lend a helping hand, Prabhakar was the opposite, being self-centreed and showing a disdain and insensitivity towards other people's woes and difficulties. Suresh wore his police uniform with pride and was a big women's advocate, encouraging young women and girls to get a good education and focus on their careers.

"Nothing. He left nothing for anyone. That is not all. I learnt about his leaving for London with Leena about a week later, around the same time that I learnt about his resignation. Prakash, my friend's son who works as a mechanic in the airport, told me he saw Prabhakar leaving with a woman on a flight to London. I guessed that it was Leena."

"I thought he had broken up with Leena a considerable time before his wedding," Suresh said.

"Well apparently, they have been in touch with each other all these years," Mamayya said. "They must have had clandestine meetings all this while." When she heard these words of Mamayya, Radha's heart contracted again and she felt that pain once more of being deceived. While she had been toiling and sweating and taking care of everyone's needs, she thought, her husband had continued his affair with Leena.

Parvathi and Arun said nothing for a long time, their faces reflecting their dismay and shock. At last Parvathi spoke up: "How are you going to manage?"

"We should be alright for the next few months," said Mamayya. "I do have a few savings."

"I think you should file a complaint and make sure that he gives child support at least." This, from Suresh.

"But he has not filed for separation or even indicated that he will not return," said Mamayya. "On what grounds are we going to ask for child or any other financial support?"

Suresh immediately took out his notebook, something he used for all his home expenses. He addressed Radha, "*Vadina* [sister-in-law], what is the monthly expense to run the house?"

Radha was stupefied. "Suresh, I never handle the money in this house. It is always Mamayya or Prabhakar who buy everything that is necessary for the house and for the children. You have seen that yourself." Whereupon Suresh nodded silently and turned to his father and asked him the same question. Mamayya and Suresh then began discussing the expenses for the children including school fees, schoolbooks and the sundry expenses of the household.

Devoid of any words of advice or comfort, Parvathi had cried quietly and embraced Radha. Radha remained stoic. The children played in the front yard, oblivious to the storm in their lives. Atthayya lay on her cot, wasted and ill, as unaware as her grandchildren. When Radha went in to get something for everyone to eat, Parvathi had followed her into the kitchen.

Radha asked her quietly, "Have you ever seen Leena, Parvathi?" She had found it hard to utter that name, Leena. "Is she very beautiful?"

Parvathi looked at her kindly and said, "Not as beautiful as you, Radha."

"You are just saying that to make me feel better. You know, Parvathi, I tried to be a good wife."

"You have been a perfect wife and a great daughter-in-law, and both my parents love you, Radha. We all love and care so much for you. You do not know how much everyone appreciates all that you do. Please do not blame yourself for what has happened. Frankly, Prabhakar doesn't deserve you. He never deserved you." With that, Parvathi had carried the tray out. At that juncture, Radha felt that fate seemed to have drawn a curtain in front of her, making it impossible to envisage the future. The only thing she could be sure about and grateful for, was the undying support of Mamayya, Parvati and Suresh.

During the first few months, Radha worried that Prabhakar would come and take the children away, tempting them with the allure of life in a foreign land, offering them comforts that she and Mamayya would never be able to provide. She had nightmares in which the children were getting into a taxi and leaving, not saying goodbye to her, not turning around to wave to her. Fortunately, that never happened.

Over the years, Radha began to view her own life as consisting of two phases, the one with Prabhakar and the other without him. How could someone you thought you knew even better than yourself just leave you and walk away? The second month following Prabhakar's departure, she was ridden with deep guilt. Her introspection led her on a path that was full of self recrimination. He would not have left them, she thought, if she had been more educated, more intelligent and beautiful. Whenever she had looked at herself in the mirror, she was reminded of her simplicity. She was riddled with a feeling of inadequacy at her multiple lapses and deficiencies, the factors that had separated her children from their father and deprived Mamayya of his son. Maybe she had not been the ideal wife. She remembered her father, an unworldly, almost naive, poor Sanskrit scholar, recounting sage Brihaspathi's definition of a pious and good wife:

*A good wife waits upon her husband, is constantly by his side like a shadow, taking care of his wants, never nagging, not trying to separate him from his parents. She eats after her husband and children eat. She attends to the needs of the entire family. A good wife does not go out alone unless it is absolutely necessary. Even when she visits her neighbours in unusual times of necessity, a good wife keeps her head bent, intent on her path, not looking up at strangers or engaging in unnecessary conversations.* But she had been all the above, she thought. She never ventured out on her own excepting when necessary. She attended to the needs of everyone excepting her own. She had subjugated any desires she may have had to the needs of the family members. The injunctions and qualities for being a good wife were endless. One night as she lay tossing and turning in the post-Prabhakar period, she suddenly realized that her father never enumerated the qualities of a good husband. It had been unbearable to be this recently deserted woman with three children, a sick mother-in-law and a father-in-law who refused to take the name of his ambitious, errant son.

Three months ago, on that unforgettable afternoon, Prabhakar and Leena's story spilled out of the cream-coloured pages. Yes, he and Leena had married and stayed on in London for three years. Leena's uncle, who was an hotelier, gave Prabhakar a job almost immediately. Later, as the business expanded to cities in the US, Prabhakar moved with Leena to Chicago. Yes, they had two sons. Two years ago, Leena had left him, taking their sons with her, to be with her father who had left India to settle down permanently in London. There was no hint of apology, no mention of wrongdoing on his part. It was the narrative of a stranger. He, Prabhakar, had decided to return to his first family. "I want to see you, Radha, you and the children. I hope that father will have no objection to my returning." He did not mention his children's names nor did he mention his mother, probably presuming her to be long since gone. How shockingly simple he made it sound. Typical of Prabhakar, taking for granted that the whole world somehow revolved around his will and wishes. After she read the letter, Radha handed it over to Mamayya. When he came to the last page, Mamayya became nearly apoplectic. He swore aloud. His swear words in Telugu, including the buffalo, the bandicoot, the snake and the donkey, resounded in the large living room. Vasu, short for Vasudev, and the eldest of Radha's children, who had just come in from his clinic, laughed aloud. "*Thathayya* [grandfather]," he asked, "who are you swearing at? Are you going up and down the evolutionary ladder?" Radha had always loved the banter between the children and their grandfather, but this evening she was much too distracted by the contents of the letter.

"Your father," replied Radha.

"My father…. Isn't it too late in the day? Sixteen years too late?" asked Vasu without even pausing, discarding his shoes at the threshold and going in to wash up.

"Guess what, Amma," he said from the inner room, "I helped deliver a baby today. The obstetrician, Dr. Nanhe, could not make it to the hospital on time. The nurse who helped me suspects that the mother of the baby is unmarried and that she will probably leave the baby with us in the hospital. Maybe the hospital and social service department will put the baby up for adoption." Momentarily, this piece of news distracted both Radha and Mamayya. Radha thought of the plight of the young mother and the circumstances leading to her wanting to give up the baby for adoption. Such stories always saddened and disappointed her, again fortifying in her mind the vagaries of human nature.

Mamayya, who seemed to have lost his train of thought at Vasu's breaking news, quickly recovered and continued on his verbal warpath. "How dare he write this letter? What gall, what insolence. Shameless man that he is. How dare he say that he wants to come back to his first family? Does he know that he broke the law when he married without getting a divorce from you?" Looking at his reaction, Radha laughed. When Prabhakar had been with them, in spite of all the chores and her household responsibilities, despite working incessantly from dawn to dusk, despite the numerous tasks at hand, despite Atthayya's illness, Radha had always found humour and happiness in almost everything. She would smile and laugh at the small incongruities of everyday life, discovering unexpected humour in what her children said and did or at the harmless eccentricities of the people around her. But she lost that sense of humour and that spark of happiness and optimism in one singular moment on that fateful day as she saw Prabhakar leaving. Sixteen years later, as she heard Mamayya complaining and cursing, the laughter bubbling from her, released her years of pain, and she felt a lightness in her heart. She even felt a little triumphant that after all this time, the man who left them years ago was asking to come back to her and the family.

"Mamayya," she exclaimed, "a man who is capable of leaving behind three children, a wife and his parents without ever writing to them or calling them is capable of a lot of other things. Remember, you once said that your son was a big risk taker? At that time, it sounded like a qualification. He broke the law and took a risk. He knew that we would not pursue him, to save ourselves embarrassment in the society. He also knew that all of us are kind and forgiving people and that we would not be vindictive with him."

"Are you willing to forgive him?" thundered Mamayya, coming and standing in front of her. Radha was quiet for what seemed an eternity. She looked up at Mamayya, at the clothes hanging loose upon his gaunt frame, his hair grey and sparse, the travails of time etched into his face. His eyes were burning embers behind his glasses, and his expression was grim. Ever since Atthayya's demise, Mamayya chose to wear only white 'khadi' clothes, as a mark of respect for his departed wife. He had refused to listen to his grandchildren who had protested against this and had tried to convince him to wear at least muted solid colours.

After what seemed an interminable pause, Radha said: "If you can forgive him, so can I, after all, he is your son."

"Well then, I can never forgive him," he said and went back to his pacing, his hands akimbo, the letter still in his hand, the papers now a little crumpled. "It is time you made a decision, Radha," he had said, then: "file for your divorce." There it was. Mamayya had finally uttered the word: divorce. Radha kept quiet. She realized he was giving her permission and even exhorting her to do something she had never planned in her wildest imagination.

"It is only symbolic, Mamayya," she replied, "we have been separated for sixteen years, longer than we had lived together."

"What's happening?" asked Vasu walking in, wiping his face and hands with a towel. The smell of sandalwood soap hung in the air, at once sublime and soothing.

"We got a letter from your father," Radha answered. Vasu stood still for a few moments, his gaze shifting from his grandfather to his mother. Radha observed him closely to look for a reaction, a hint of his feelings. Did he still love his father after all these years, this sensitive, loving child of hers? Amongst her three children, perhaps, Vasu's memory of his father would be the strongest. Prabhakar had left one Sunday, at eight in the morning after Mamayya had gone on an errand. The three children clung to her as they watched Prabhakar get into the taxi. Vasu had been nine, Mukund, six and Sunanda, four. Memory was a strange thing, she thought, even small fragments of it having a tensile strength to bind people. Memory was like the strong vines she grew in her nursery, some of which grasped at the trellises or big trees, binding to them with an annealing desire so powerful that after a few months or years it was impossible to separate them. Sometimes, she thought that Vasu had surpassed her and Mamayya in terms of maturity, tolerance and an understanding of the human condition and human foibles. How wonderful the three children had been, thought Radha. They had been so easy to raise and guide, with very few tantrums or demands. The three of them seemed to have understood the dire state of their circumstances, saving her and Mamayya the pain and ordeal of ever having to explain to them why certain things available to other children from wealthier families could not be procured for them, why they had to make do with the few clothes they had or a pair of shoes or footwear until they outgrew them or until they were beyond use and repair, why a vacation in an exciting place during the summer school holidays was not a luxury they could afford. Even after they had attained financial stability thanks to the nursery, the three of them had shown great restraint about acquiring new clothes or new gadgets. When she finally started giving them money for their individual expenses, they had exercised caution about spending it. Vasu, with a child's innate ability to capture adult life nuances, stopped asking her about his father after the first six months. One day, Vasu and she had gone for a walk, choosing the same path they always did. The government had suddenly decided to plant small saplings by the roadside as an apology for all the deforestation that had been going on in the surrounding areas. There were small wire cages around the saplings put up by the government gardeners to protect them from the occasional stray goat that wandered away from a herd. She sat on a large rock under the old tamarind tree, which had miraculously escaped the government's chain saw. The tamarind tree stood like a sentinel at the fork in the un-tarred country road. If one took the wider road to the right, it joined the highway after two hundred yards. The highway extended through the mountains to the city and from there connected to the national highway. This was the road of ambition, thought Radha. The narrow road to the left meandered its way through the nearby hamlets, running by small marigold fields, rose gardens and jasmine shrubs. There were a few small ponds along this path with floating pink and white lilies. She thought of this as the philosopher's road, a road on which a Buddha or a mendicant would prefer to walk, a road of contemplation, introspection and self discovery. From where she sat, she could see the distant mountains forming the edge of the valley. Suddenly, she heard Vasu calling out to her, his high childish voice breaking the evening's calm.

"Look, Amma. Come and see what I have found."

She rushed to where he was crouched next to a short bush and saw a fallen bird's nest. A knot of sparrows were chirping loudly on a nearby tree. She squatted by her son's side, looking at the carefully collected and arranged shreds of straw and twigs. What a beautiful nest it was, a perfectly built home that had fallen. A small egg, showing a crack in its speckled veneer, had been dislodged out of the nest, lying there upon a patch of dried grass. She picked up the little broken egg with its shell appearing almost pink in the setting sun. The loud agitated chirping of the sparrows, Radha felt, was her own inner cry of despair. As she put the little broken egg back on its bed of straw, she had burst into uncontrollable sobs. Vasu had clung to her, trying to console her while he too wept, wiping her eyes with his hands, and wiping his own with the edge of her saree. For a long time, they clung to one another, mother and son, crying over a fallen bird's nest, seeing themselves as pieces of that shattered egg. On the way home, Vasu sobbed as he recounted the number of times he had gone furtively to the post office in search of the unwritten letters from his father. In a strange, unexpected manner, this one incident bound them together. Radha saw once again the sensitive, caring nature of Vasu, his childish vulnerability, and felt the recurrent pain of how uncaring Prabhakar had been towards his children. They carried home the fallen nest with its egg that evening. In the backyard at the edge of the fence, they dug a small hole in which they reverentially placed the remains of that egg. Radha felt that a part of her body and a part of her soul were in that shattered egg. Vasu placed the bird's nest in a corner of the low roof over the veranda at the front of the house, balancing it carefully over the broad rafters. When his brother and sister asked him what he was doing, he replied that he was keeping a nest ready for the sparrows. He called it "a nest for rent." Radha smiled at his ability to bring some levity to the sad incident.

As she gazed at Vasu, who was now looking at the envelope in which his father's letter had arrived, she saw not a young man on the threshold of life and its big adventure, but a boy of nine who had wept over a fallen bird's nest containing its fragile egg and had tried to console his mother. In Radha's eyes, he was still the young boy who had confessed about his trips to the post office for his father's unwritten letters. When they had moved to the new house, Vasu had carried the bird's nest from the old dilapidated house, and when his brother and sister made fun of him, he had explained: "This bird's nest is my anchor in life. It will always keep me rooted to the ground, to what reality is."

"Pray, do tell us what 'reality' is," they had teased him.

"I will tell you one day," he answered somberly, mysteriously, like a philosopher who had discovered the secret of life. At times, Radha suspected that Vasu along with his grandfather did not divulge everything going on in their worlds. Perhaps they had secrets, which they did not share with her to protect her from getting hurt or worried, or maybe even this suspicion on her part was a result of her own imagination. Mamayya stopped in front of Vasu and said, "Your long-lost father wants to come back to us, to you all, to your mother whom he deserted many years ago without a backward glance." Before Vasu could react, Mamayya went back to his pacing. Radha's gaze was fixed upon Vasu.

"Well, Thathayya," he said, "it's up to Amma to decide, isn't it? But why, after all these years, does he want us? Does he know how well Amma has done for herself and for all of us?" Then, he turned to Radha, addressing her, "Amma, whatever decision you make, I will be with you." He came to her, kneeling by her chair, holding both her hands in his. Looking up at her, he said with conviction: "I do not care to see him or speak with him. If you want to have him back, then so be it. But showing him respect or love is going to be difficult for me."

"I want your grandfather to be also involved in this decision. It is to do with his son after all."

"I think you should just ignore this letter and let us live in peace," Mamayya had responded.

"How can we ignore it?" Radha had asked. "Some kind of action is necessary on our part." A week after the letter arrived, Radha had penned a response in Telugu, her mother tongue, their mother tongue, and not in English as Prabhakar had done. She initially wanted Vasu or Mamayya to respond to Prabhakar's letter, but after vehement refusals from them both, she had no choice but to do it herself. It had been over a weekend when they had all congregated together in the large living room. Contrary to Prabhakar's letter—which ran for five pages, each page embossed with his name and address, phone numbers, signs of his success and money—her reply to the letter had been startlingly brief, direct and telegraphic. She avoided addressing him. She did not choose the paper with the nursery's letterhead, instead, preferring a plain white one. *We (not I) received your letter. You can contact us (not me) when you arrive in India.* "Which address should I give? Or should I give our phone number?" Radha had asked of no one in particular. There was a chorus of suggestions and warnings from the children.

"If you give the home address, he may come here directly," this from Mukund.

Radha smiled at Mukund's response. He was one year out of law school and already behaved like a seasoned lawyer, she thought, always a step ahead of others, attuned to the frailties of humans, anticipating, judging their behaviours and making plans to counter their next moves.

"Perhaps the post office would be good. The people in the post office know us." This was from Vasu.

"Just give him our office phone number," Sunanda suggested. Finally, they decided that the office phone number and the address of the post office would be the best. She had sealed the envelope and left it to Vasu to mail it. Prabhakar's letter had been like a sudden gale pounding on a ship sailing peacefully on the seas, making it veer from its path. The letter had thrown them into turmoil, and every once in a while, during the ensuing weeks, Radha could sense the anxiety in the three children and in Mamayya. Her children were adults now, and she was proud of the way they had turned out. Vasu had graduated from medical school and was finishing his internship. Sunanda would be graduating from college in a year and wanted to pursue pharmacology as a career.

This afternoon, as she continued to lean against the tree, her outstretched hand drawing succor from the imprint of the rough, broken bark on her palm, Tony pulled the little rattan stool that he always kept in the trunk, which, though it looked frail, was very strong and coaxed Radha to sit upon it. He then got a bottle of water and brought it to her. "Amma, please have some water. You will feel better." Whenever he addressed her as "Amma," she relished being so addressed, "Mother." This evening though, she had a lot on her mind and was not in the real mood to dwell upon the common and banal pleasures of the everyday. She was very nervous, confused and a little resentful that the whole family had left her to face Prabhakar alone. She wished she had a book or a guide that told her how to handle this situation. They had a book on most things these days—how to make your breakfast, lunch and dinner, how to discipline your children, how to deal with demanding parents and parents-in-law, how to break in a pet dog or cat, how to manage an aquarium or aviary at home, how to deal with an unexpected guest—but no tome on how to deal with a spouse who wanted to return to the family after being absent for years. Perhaps, she thought, she could have got legal counsel, but this was Mamayya's son, her children's father, and the thought of legal recourse had never crossed her mind. She wished she had a best friend, someone who was a dear confidante, wise and strong, there by her side, at this very difficult hour. But she had been isolated from most social interactions excepting those related to business all these years. She had felt a sense of shame at the abandonment by Prabhakar and had subjected herself into a self-imposed isolation. She had been thirty-five years old when Prabhakar left. At the beginning, she had even shunned most of the parent day activities in her children's school and the local festivities, always choosing the excuse that her nursery took a lot of her time. The first few years had been the most difficult. On the rare occasion when she would venture to the market to buy supplies for the house or her nursery, she wondered and worried if there were people around her who knew that her husband had left her and her children and had walked out of their lives. She thought of imaginary fingers pointed at her, unsympathetic whispers and the accusations that perhaps the entire fault had been hers, which is why her husband had left. It was so true, she had thought at that time, that the woman was always deemed responsible when such things happened. That worry and threat of ostracism had kept her confined to the house and her work. She had also worried about her children being teased at school for being fatherless. Luckily, that had not happened, or if it had, they had not told her, and they seemed quite content and unafraid to go to school. There had been one evening, though, when Mukund had returned from playing with some of the neighbourhood boys. He was sullen and quiet. Radha had been at the kitchen counter preparing dinner. She stopped what she was doing and, taking him in her arms, coaxed him to tell her what the matter was, and he had asked her where his father was. Before she could respond, he continued: "All my friends were talking about what each of their fathers did and when they asked me, I had no answer." Radha had replied that, should that question arise, he should hereafter just tell everyone that his father was in England on some business. At that juncture, in fact, that is all she knew about Prabhakar. After that, there seemed to have been no trouble with awkward questions for the children.

Now, sitting upon the stool, Radha wiped the perspiration from her face with a trembling hand and drank some water. Tony then spread a small mat and sat down by her feet. Gently he released her feet from her sandals and started rubbing them, assuring her that she was going to be all right. Radha tried to stop him, saying that a foot rub was not necessary, but he would not listen. He put both her feet on his lap, ignoring her words, and took out a small bottle of oil from his pocket and, opening it, poured a few drops of it on his palms and starting massaging her feet.

"I didn't know that you carried this bottle with you," she remarked, looking down gratefully at Tony, glad that she had listened to everyone's suggestion that it was he who should accompany her. After all, she told everyone that he was her third son.

"I always carry this, Amma," he replied, looking up at her and smiling. "I have done this often for Sir [meaning Mamayya], and he likes this." Tony lived with them and had become one of the family. Radha had made sure that he had his own room in the spacious house that they had built and enjoyed all the creature comforts that she and the rest of the family did. After a few minutes of silence, Tony spoke up again: "Amma, I learnt this from my grandmother. Whenever any of us was tired or agitated, she would make us sit down and then rub our feet with a little oil. She said that this helped to soothe one's nerves." Tony was a big fellow and unusually gentle with everyone. He had arrived one rainy evening, completely lost, on a beaten down cycle, seeking shelter at their equally beaten down house. By that time, Prabhakar had been gone for several years. Tony's name was not Tony. As he related his story, once he became more familiar with everyone, the time he had spent with them slowly allowing him to let his guard down, his real name was Tirupati, a name given to him after the city of the seven hills, close to the village where he was born and raised and where his family still lived. After high school, he had worked in a local convent as a janitor. "The convent sisters were very kind," he said. The first day, when he rang the bell at the large gate of the convent, he was taken to Sister Alphonso. "Now, why would anyone have the name of a mango?" Tony asked. As soon as Sister Mango, as Tony nicknamed her, asked him for his name, he decided to say on an impulse, "Tony." "She was very fair," Tony said, by way of explanation, "and looked like a foreigner, maybe from England or America. I thought of an easy name that she and the rest of the sisters would be able to pronounce and the first name that came to my mind was Tony." He had worked in the convent for two years, and during those years, he had learnt to speak English well and to help with some of the accounts for Sister Alphonso, alias Sister "Mango." It was Sister Mango who had encouraged Tony to read the newspapers, saying that newspaper reading would improve his language skills. He also read some old Reader's Digest issues that he found in one of the storage rooms of the convent. He decided to move to a larger township to increase his earnings in order to help his family. He had endeared himself to Radha, Mamayya and the children with his hard work and dedication. He even took upon himself extra chores when necessary.

His hands, surprisingly soft and warm, kneaded her feet, coaxing the muscles to relax. He stretched the joints by pulling on her toes. Radha looked down at her own hands, her nails cut short, with no nail polish, rough and calloused over the years by all the work in the nursery. Tony focused on her feet like a Zen artist who, oblivious to the world, is centred on the task at hand. It was as though her feet were the centre of his world and nothing else mattered. He began running his fist along her soles gently at first and then with more strength. She felt her feet turn into sponge that took different shapes under his expert hands and began to relax, her breathing coming back to normal, her heart slowing down, her stomach quiet. The smell of the eucalyptus oil he was using was mild and comforting. She closed her eyes shutting out the bright light of the late afternoon.

"Perhaps this is not a good idea, my going to meet him?" she said aloud.

"What if he showed up on your doorstep, Amma, without warning, what would you do then?" asked Tony. Tony had been present at all their recent discussions concerning the impending return of Prabhakar. Although he had not spoken up during the meetings, he had listened attentively to what each member of the family had to say. After a few minutes of silence, he said, "If he shows up on your doorstep, it would be impossible to turn him away, Amma. You, of all people, would not be able to turn him away." Radha wondered if she appeared that weak, that spineless, that intimidated by a man who had not been around for the last sixteen years. Tony continued, "You would probably ask him to stay out of the kindness of your heart, maybe for a few days. What if the few days stretched into weeks and months? What if everyone was unhappy? There would be a lot of tension and worry in the family. This is the only way, Amma, the better way."

"Wouldn't the children want him back? Or Mamayya, for that matter? He was his father's favourite. Mamayya was always so proud of him. They shared a special bond."

"Even special bonds can be broken by deceit, Amma," said Tony, "and they can be destroyed forever by all the pain that was inflicted. Did Vasu, Mukund or Sunanda ever say that they wanted to meet him?" he asked. That was true, Radha had to agree. The children had not expressed any interest or curiosity in meeting their father. Rather, their attitude ever since the fateful letter arrived had been one of caution, disdain, doubt and skepticism. The three of them appeared to be endowed with a worldly wisdom that she herself did not possess at their age, Radha thought.

"You sound so wise and experienced." Tony did not respond to this. Instead he continued to rub and massage her feet. A light wind had set in, dislodging some leaves from the tree, the smell of the neem leaves distinct and almost antiseptic. They could hear the chirping of the birds gathered overhead, camouflaged by the tree branches.

"You know, Amma," Tony said, "my grandfather left my grandmother and their five children one night, taking all the money they had saved. He even took the only gold chain, something my grandmother had been given by her mother, her only insurance against hard times. And he stole the two cows; grandmother used to sell the milk from the cows to the neighbourhood families to make some money and buy the rice and vegetables with. He nearly destroyed the family." Radha was still as she listened to Tony's story. Tony continued, "Next morning when they woke up, grandmother realized that they had practically nothing to live on. The oldest child, my father, was only twelve, and the youngest was five." Radha momentarily forgot her own situation.

"What did she do? What did they do?"

"Luckily, they had a company building a large garment factory barely a mile away. Grandmother immediately went to a few of her neighbours, borrowed a little money and started a small roadside business. It was a shack, really. Every day, she would get up at daybreak, cook a large amount of food that she then wrapped up in plantain leaves to keep the food fresh and tasty, and took them to the shack from where she would sell them to the construction workers and once the factory was built and running, to the garment workers who worked there. If a worker did not have money to buy lunch—for all of them worked on daily wages—she would give him the food for free and in this way earned a lot of good will from everybody. The poor always remember kindness, Amma. This kindness and generosity were the investment she made. She churned up fresh buttermilk every morning after putting salt and lime juice in it, and she distributed it for free. While growing up, I used to drink that buttermilk made by her, and it is still the most delicious buttermilk I have ever had. Soon, there were people not connected with the garment factory, workers from other small local businesses, who started stopping at the shack for lunch. Within three months, she got one more assistant apart from my father. My father had dropped out of school to help grandmother. They did so well that soon she was selling the same packets of food from home. In two years, she set up a small restaurant close to the factory, with tables and chairs and a proper roof and a big kitchen. Then she sent my father back to school. She insisted that her children get the basic education she herself had not been fortunate enough to get and told them that it was the only way they could make something of themselves in this world."

"And what about your grandfather?"

Tony laughed. He was putting her sandals back on her feet and getting up, rolling the mat.

"Yes, Amma, I am coming to that. So, one day, almost six years later, my grandfather shows up at their doorstep, like a bad penny. My father was eighteen and had already finished his high school. He was training to be a car mechanic because that is what he wanted to be. He had dreamt of owning his own mechanic shop. He was—he still is—very good at repairing cars, tuning engines, or taking an old engine out of a car and building a new engine. Grandmother called her brother who worked in the local Tahsildar's office and had a quiet word with him. That evening, grandmother's brother and a few of his cronies took grandfather away, to all intents and purposes for celebrating his return. They made sure that he never returned or bothered my grandmother or her children again."

"What did they do? Did they beat him? Did they kill him?"

"Oh no, Amma. From what I heard, they put the fear of the devil in him and told him that if he ever returned to those parts, they will turn him over to the police for theft or they would all collectively thrash him and then parade him in the village. My grandmother led a very peaceful life after that."

They were back in the car. Radha realized that Tony's story had not only helped to calm her down, it had also prompted her to think of her options. In many ways it resonated with her own. Yes, the easiest would be to allow Prabhakar back into her life and their lives, to let him assimilate with them and get to know his children better. But was Prabhakar capable of bonding with his children? She could not recall any particular act of affection or love from him towards the children when he was with them. Yes, he had dropped the two boys at school every morning. In the evenings, they would walk home. She could not ever remember Prabhakar taking them out for a movie or to a restaurant or even to the local fairgrounds. He had been distant as a father and not very demonstrative or even affectionate. At that time, it did not seem strange to Radha because her own father had been the same with her and her brother. If a father had not bonded with his children when they were young, where was the guarantee that he would when they were all grown up, especially after sixteen years of absence? The other option was to tell him clearly that he was not welcome in their lives anymore. But she also wanted Mamayya to weigh in on this matter. After all, she felt, she alone did not have the exclusive privilege of making such a decision. Mamayya had the right to decide whether he wanted his errant son back in the fold. She reflected on what she would have done had one of her own children—Vasu or Mukund, even Sunanda—left home in a fit of anger or due to some other compelling reason and then wanted to return after several years to the family. She would willingly and eagerly welcome her child back without any questions.

Was Tony sending her a veiled message with his story? She thought of Tony's grandfather stealing his wife's gold necklace, the cows and all the money. The news that Prabhakar had closed his bank account was akin to his closing his door on one chapter of his life. A chapter in which she, the three children, Mamayya and Athhayya lived. That he had not had the generosity to leave some money for his father, who he knew was struggling with his floundering garment business, stunned her. The money Prabhakar had taken with him had been a substantial amount. True, it was his money and perhaps none of them, including Mamayya, had any claims over it. She was still shocked and dismayed that he did not leave anything, if not for her, at least for the children, their school, education and books. He owed that much to the children as their father. Even after all these years when she thought about it, she felt a great sadness for her children, that they had been deprived at an early age of the love, support and guidance of a father. She, Radha, had never had a bank account up to that time, nor had she seen the necessity for it. As long as she had she lived with her parents, they had provided for her every need. When she was working as a typist before she married, she had given her entire salary, a pittance by today's standards, to her mother so that she could use it for the house. She remembered how, a few months after Prabhakar had left, they were short of cash, and she gave Mamayya her gold chain to sell so that they could buy the medicines for Atthayya. Mamayya had been adamant about not selling a woman's property, or *streedhan*, as he termed it. He said: "I will borrow from Suresh or Parvathi."

"Mamayya, you know how expensive life is in the city," Radha reminded him, "and Suresh and Nirmala have incurred so much debt with the house they recently bought." She continued, "And you know that Parvathi and her husband have big plans for their children's education." This was true. Parvathi's son was taking all the exams for entrance to an engineering college, and her daughter, who was older, had just begun her postgraduate course. She had finally convinced Mamayya to sell the gold and remembered how his hands shook and his lips trembled with suppressed emotion as he took the chain from her. "Mamayya, please do not feel bad about this. We can always buy gold, maybe a better gold chain in the future." He looked at her as though she was slightly delusional. Later, as their hardships continued, she had sold her gold bangles as well. Tony's story had roused a cornucopia of old and unhappy memories. It was a few months after she started the nursery that she finally opened her own bank account. Mamayya accompanied her to the bank, which was two miles away, and it had been on a monsoon afternoon. She had been leaving the money she made from the nursery in a cardboard box standing on the kitchen counter. She had hurriedly stuffed all the notes into a cloth bag without counting them and gone on the scooter to the bank, riding on the pillion, clutching the cloth bag. There were roadside puddles and the road was wet and slippery. Mamayya was not used to riding the scooter, and it was a wobbly ride during which she was scared that she or he or both of them would at any minute tumble from the vehicle. The water and mud from the tires of the scooter got on her feet and sandals and saree and onto Mamayya's clothes. The bank agent who helped them stared at them, his mouth open in shock, when she emptied the cloth bag, the notes spilling on his table. The three of them, Mamayya, the bank officer and she, counted the money. There were thousands of rupees. She felt elation at the amount earned by her and was at the same time embarrassed that she had been that careless about the money. On the way home, they stopped at a small coffee shop and she and Mamayya celebrated this singular milestone with some snacks and hot steaming coffee. That dangerous heart-stopping journey inspired Radha to learn riding the scooter herself. Vasu helped her, making sure she did not lose her balance and fall. It was quite an effort, but she managed to master the scooter and was soon able to get her licence. Thereafter, she always drove the scooter, and one of the children or Mamayya would ride on the pillion if they had to run errands especially for the nursery. On some days, if it were a matter of one or two potted plants that needed to be delivered, she would take them with her on the scooter. For larger orders, they hired a van driver. Owning a car and a van came much later.

Tony drove smoothly, his eyes fixed on the road, a picture of alertness and concentration. They took the exit from the highway and were nearing the restaurant. The highway ran almost parallel to the exit road for a kilometre before becoming serpiginous, weaving up the mountains on the other side of which was the city. On the radio, she heard devotional songs in praise of Lord Hanuman. Without her asking, Tony said, "It is Lord Hanuman's birthday today. They are having a night long event in the temple."

"Maybe we should have selected another day; the restaurant may be very busy and crowded."

"It won't be crowded now, Amma, perhaps later in the evening."

Radha wondered if there was any residuum of affection in her for Prabhakar, the father of her children. They were unequivocally her children now; of that she was clear. Was she still a little in awe of him, perhaps, because of the perception— her perception—of his superior intelligence? She was so unsure. She remembered her beautiful relationship with Atthaya and how much she had made her feel welcome in the home when she arrived as a new bride. Radha had learnt almost everything about running a household from Athhayya, who had herself been from a very poor family. At the time that Prabhakar left, Athhayya's health was steadily deteriorating, her food intake decreasing, her energy on the decline like the setting sun or waning moon. It was the last lap of her sojourn upon this earth. Dr. Ramakanth, the kind doctor from the municipality clinic, would pay a weekly visit and check her with his stethoscope and blood pressure apparatus. He would look at her eyes and nails as she lay upon her cot in the small bedroom. She was unaware of Prabhakar's absence. The only time she responded was when little Sunanda climbed up on the cot, lay there hugging her grandmother. Then a small, tremulous smile would play upon her lips. When they saw her smile this way, they would all have tears in their eyes, Radha, Mamayya, Parvathi and Suresh. Atthayya's demise a few months later had left a terrible void. It was only after she died that it occurred to her how heartless and selfish Prabhakar had been. Luckily, Suresh and Parvathi were there with them for two whole weeks until all the ceremonies and rituals were over. At times, Radha felt that Mamayya, Suresh and Parvathi felt more guilt than she herself about Prabhakar's leaving. Suresh visited them every other weekend, often times alone, at other times with his wife and two children, a boy and a girl who were the same ages as hers, and seeing them play together made her happy and for a while forget all her worries. She was glad that through all these years, Suresh and Parvathi's children and her own had maintained a close bond and affection.

# Kamalnath and the Restaurant

Radha's thoughts were momentarily interrupted when she realized that they were arriving at their destination. The red tiled roof of the restaurant could be seen over the treetops. Adjacent to the restaurant and towering over it, was the Hanuman mountain, with the temple of Lord Hanuman sitting on top, a triangular orange flag fluttering over the tower. Radha could see the Bougainvillea, red, orange and white flanking the thirty steps leading to the temple. At the beginning, the restaurant had been more like a large hut, with a tumultuous array of dried palm leaves for a roof, supported on brick pillars with thirty rickety tables that stood in disarray under wooden beams from which hung sixty-watt electric bulbs from hollow steel rods, with the short black insulated wire projecting an inch below the end of the rods. Heavy mats were rolled up to the ceiling around the dining area, and these would be put down periodically when it was too gusty or too hot. Despite its disoriented appearance, there had always been a sense of light and air and optimism in the restaurant. The thatched roof of the restaurant balanced precariously over the pillars—or at least precariousness was the impression it gave, with its slight asymmetry and tilt, ever in perpetual danger of being blown away by a strong wind. Folks believed that it was the divine power of Lord Hanuman, the ruling deity in the temple atop the mountain, who endowed the restaurant with its invincibility against the vile forces and vagaries of Mother Nature. As times and fortunes changed and the restaurant became a more profitable venture, Kamalnath, the owner of the restaurant, had made several improvements. The short brick wall had been replaced by a proper stone wall and the thatched roof replaced by red tiles, and now fluorescent lights hung from an elaborately designed beam ceiling. In a way, the life of the restaurant and her own, as well as that of her family, had a shared trajectory, Radha thought, progressing from near extinction to becoming a durable and successful venture. She quickly checked her bag to see if she had her phone with her.

"Call me as soon as you reach the restaurant," Mamayya had told her. She had nodded silently. The family had debated as to the best day and time that the meeting should take place. It had been Mamayya who had suggested this particular evening. Everyone agreed that the evening time in the middle of the week would be very good. It would be quieter. The restaurant did get very busy on Thursdays, Fridays and the weekends. The idea of inviting Prabhakar over to the house was never brought up by anyone. They had chosen the restaurant as the meeting place because Radha felt at home and comfortable in the restaurant. Ever since it opened fifteen years ago, she had been providing plants from the nursery to the restaurant, and she had also undertaken the responsibility for the upkeep of the garden at the front and the vegetable plants and fruit trees in the back. Over the years, Kamalnath and his wife Malathi had become family friends. The tables in the restaurant were evenly spaced with enough distance between them to allow for privacy. As the van slowed, she looked to see if there were other vehicles parked there. She hoped Prabhakar had not come early like her.

She asked Tony to pull the van into the small gravel path leading away from the driveway and to park behind the little tumulus created when the restaurant had undergone all the remodelling. Getting out of the van, she asked him to seek the shade of the spreading mango tree a little behind the tumulus. If he decided to wait in the van for her, Radha thought, it would be cooler under the tree than the outside, with the windows of the van rolled down. She mentioned this to him as the alternative to sitting outside, in the dry heat of the little valley. Laughing his customary laugh, Tony said, "Amma, do not worry about me. I'll be fine in the van or outside. Besides, I have brought my fan with me." He showed her the tattered palm leaf fan that he always carried with him. It was made of interwoven dried palm leaves attached to a foot long flat stick, much like a flag. There were wide gaps between the palm leaves now, making it ineffective as a fan. Every time she saw it, Radha would remark that he should replace it and each time she got the same response: "No, Amma, I've had it for many years. I brought it from my village." Every time, Radha would simply shake her head and smile.

As soon as she entered the cool shade of the restaurant, Kamalnath rushed to her with his characteristic long strides, smiling, joining his hands in a greeting and accompanying her to her table. He was a tall man, towering over most people, and she had to look up at him as they spoke. Mamayya had already forewarned Kamalnath about the purpose of her visit this afternoon and Kamalnath had assured him that he and his wife would be there, ready with any help that Radha needed. She had always preferred the table at the farthest corner in the restaurant. It was peaceful in the corner and gave her a good view of the garden and the fountain through the large open windows and provided a vantage point to observe the people coming in and leaving. Kamalnath left after a few pleasantries and making sure she was seated comfortably. Kamalnath had ventured into the restaurant business twice in the past. The first time, it was in the city, but his business had soon succumbed to fierce competition in spite of the fact that he and his wife were good chefs. Malathi had gone to a culinary school and had also trained in the hospitality industry, and they had been so sure of success. Six months later, he and Malathi started a small eatery attached to a grocery store, but the grocery store closed after one year and the number of people stopping for the ready made and take out food dwindled slowly over the course of three months. Kamalnath then decided that he should probably look into other business ventures. He had his four children to support as well as his parents, who lived with them, and a younger brother still in college. Then, one night, he recounted, Lord Hanuman appeared in his dream. The next day, as a response to the divine calling, he went to visit the Hanuman temple to appease this God. While returning from the temple, climbing down the steps, he saw a generous stretch of land that was for sale right next to the mountain. Kamalnath was convinced it was a direct message from Lord Hanuman. He bought the piece of land with the money he had saved and started building his restaurant.

Being an ardent devotee of Lord Hanuman, he wanted to name the restaurant "The Hanuman Hotel" after his favourite deity. The priests and trustees of the temple objected. "We do not want people to associate the hotel with the temple and then be under the wrong impression that the temple owns the hotel."

So that was that. Kamalnath, being a pious man and not wanting to cause displeasure to the temple establishment and its trustees, abandoned the name "The Hanuman Hotel." Kamalnath's astrologer had told him that the most propitious syllables for the name, considering the restaurant's north-facing entrance and Kamalnath's birth star, would be *Ho, Hee, Ma* or *Fa*. Of course, if all the syllables were incorporated into the name, the hotel would become invincible like Lord Hanuman himself. It was a sore temptation, to become as invincible as this God with a manly frame, the face of a monkey and a powerful tail that had even lifted a mountain. After due consideration and a family ballot, which involved close to thirty-five kith and kin of Kamalnath, the name "Hotel Highway Very Most Famous" was coined. Malathi's brother had suggested that, as the restaurant was close to the highway, it should be called Hotel Highway. Everyone applauded that. Kamalnath's older brother said adding the word "Famous" would be a good idea. There were enthusiastic nods all around. Kamalnath's father-in-law said adding the words "very most" would endow the name with a greater punch, something unforgettable. According to Kamalnath, this was a pure stroke of genius. The name became "Hotel Highway Very Most Famous." Promptly, a colourful satin banner bearing the name of the restaurant went up.

Lakshman, the oldest waiter working there, the one who had been with Kamalnath and his enterprise from the very beginning, hurried towards Radha, his customary clean white towel upon his shoulder, his glasses, as always, nearly falling off his nose and his well-oiled hair swept back. The only thing that kept Lakshman's glasses from falling off his nose, her children often joked, was the divine power of Lord Hanuman. In many ways, Lakshman so resembled Mamayya that Radha found some solace in his presence.

They had had a "Prabhakar plebiscite," as Vasu phrased it, more than a week ago on a Sunday. Suresh and Parvati were also present. Parvathi, who had felt very passionately about the callousness exhibited by Prabhakar towards Radha and the children, was very vociferous and vetoed any idea of allowing Prabhakar back. "Where is the guarantee that he will not leave you again?" she asked.

Suresh, being a policeman, was suspicious about Prabhakar wanting to reunite with his "first" family. "The whole idea reeks of something suspicious. He may try to claim the nursery and the house if given a chance," Suresh said. Radha had not considered this possibility.

"Why would he be interested in the nursery or the house, for that matter? He has his hotels to manage and seems to be quite prosperous," was Radha's response.

Mukund, the most outspoken of the three children, said, "Amma, I do not know why you are doing this. Please don't do this for us. I don't need a stranger as a father in my life. If you are doing it for Thathayya or yourself, then please go ahead. I will accept your decision." Vasu had been more circumspect as always, reiterating that he would abide by any decision she made. Sunanda had tears in her eyes, choking back her sobs as she finally burst out after many years of silence, "Who does he think he is, trying to claim a place in our lives, in our hearts, after all these years? Do you know how much I longed for a father to be by my side at the most important moments in my life? Where was he then? I hope this is not an imposter, Amma."

Radha was taken aback by this emotional outburst from her daughter and had got up from her seat, went and hugged Sunanda, feeling the pain and anguish that her daughter had bottled up all these years. She then made Sunanda sit next to her and comforted her. There was some truth in Sunanda's remark about a potential imposter, for the newspapers in the past few years had been rife with all sorts of stories—forgotten wives, husbands, brothers and sons turning up and turning the lives of everyone involved upside down. Two years ago, there was a long-running court battle between an alleged returning son and the parent family. The purported son was an exact replica of the son who had gone missing fifteen years ago, and the local newspapers had daily information including the old and recent photos, a picture depicting the police projection of what the son would look like after fifteen years, the childhood amulet worn by the returning son and finally the DNA test results. Those cautionary words from Sunanda elicited vigorous head nodding from the boys, whereupon Mamayya responded sardonically, "Do not worry, it is not that easy to pose as someone as stupid as your father." The three children had gotten back spiritedly at their grandfather. "Please do not call him our father. He lost that title many years ago." To this response and the glares accompanying it, Mamayya laughed heartily. Once in a while, he liked to rile the children in this manner, rousing their ire. This in turn elicited laughter from him, the privilege of being a grandparent. Parvathi and Suresh had joined in the laughter. This was the first time they were openly discussing the absent Prabhakar after so many years. As they sat there in the large comfortable living room which she and the children had so painstakingly organised and decorated, Radha realized that it was as though they had all made a pact of never bringing up the topic of their absent father all these years, perhaps as a considerate gesture towards her. Her heart ached when she thought of the void the three had experienced growing up. However, the presence of Mamayya had to a large part assuaged this void, this deficiency of an absent father. Suresh, too, had tried to fill the role of the absent Prabhakar, accompanying the children on important occasions to the school or on other outings when Radha had been tied up with her work. Ever since Prabhakar left, Mamayya had been with them constantly, even refusing to go and spend a few days with Suresh who repeatedly invited him to visit him and his family in the city. Once, when she had asked Mamayya, why he did not visit Suresh, suggesting that it would be a good change for him, Mamayya had replied that his place was here with them and that the children should never feel the lack of a father figure, not even for a single day. Her heart ached, too, for the loss Mamayya had experienced, first with the absence of Prabhakar and then with the demise of Atthayya.

As she sat at the table, Radha wished again that Mamayya or one of the children were with her to boost her confidence. They had steadfastly held the argument that this was a meeting between a husband and wife, where there was no room for a third person, and that whatever decision she made today should not be influenced by their presence. Moreover, they said that if all of them showed up, it may lead Prabhakar to think that it was a reception committee that had come to welcome him back into their lives, and that would be sending the wrong message. No, she as his wife (still) had to make that decision. After all, they argued, Prabhakar had reached out to her and not to his father or his children, asking to come back to them.

She made a quick phone call to Mamayya telling him she had reached the restaurant and put the phone back in her bag. She leant against the chair and took a deep breath, wondering if she would be able to recognise Prabhakar after all these years. He had had the audacity to send photographs of his house, a large hotel he owned and one photograph of himself with his first letter. In the photograph, he was leaning against a gray van, with mountains in the backdrop. The cap he wore had left most of his face in the shadow. All she could see was a moustache. He always had a bit of showmanship, and it now came to the fore in the way he crossed his legs, his apparently expensive shoes, shining brown in the autumn sunlight, his arms crossed across his little potbelly. She could tell it was autumn from the colours of the leaves in the photograph. In America, autumn is called "fall." This snippet of information was one of many she had gathered over the years from her children. When she showed the photograph to the children they had all commented in their own unique way. Sunanda, being the fashionable young woman that she was, commented that his hat, shirt and trousers were not very coordinated. Vasu commented on the shadows covering his face and on the moustache.

"Did he have a moustache, Amma, I mean when he left us?"

"No," answered Radha.

"Hmm," this from Mukund, disapprovingly, "all that is missing is a pipe. Is he trying to project himself as some type of a tycoon? Or a man about town, showing off his prosperity?"

Mamayya looked at the photograph and threw it down on the table with disdain. He was quiet. Radha knew how much Mamayya had doted upon Prabhakar, the one with the best looks and intelligence, well regarded by everyone. They had shared a close bond, father and son, and often they would go for walks on those evenings that Prabhakar returned early from the college he used to teach at. They had cherished each other's company, discussing a variety of topics, with Prabhakar giving his father the latest local, national and international news. This, in a way, had helped to fill the lacuna that Mamayya felt from his own lack of higher education, as he had dropped out of the second year of college to help his own father run the garment shop. After his father had died, he had continued the business out of necessity and out of a certain sense of loyalty to his father's memory and enterprise. He also did it for the five employees in the shop who depended on it for their livelihood. He had been encouraging his workers to find other employment since he was aware that soon the day would come when he would have to give up this business, as the returns had decreased every year due to the competition from the ready-made garment industry, as more and more people preferred to go to shops selling ready-made clothes, not inclined any more to go and buy cloth to get it stitched by a tailor. At the time that Prabhakar left, only two employees, old timers nearing retirement age, were still working in the shop. A few days after Atthayya's passing away, Mamayya had finally sold his shop for a pittance. Looking back now, Radha wondered how they had survived those hard, desperate times. Her own parents were no more, and her only sibling, a brother older than her by six years, had not been very communicative or affectionate and had moved away even before her wedding. Whatever sorrow or despair she felt, she had bottled inside, not wanting to upset the children or Mamayya. Commiserating with someone had not been an option. One night, after the children had gone to bed, she was putting away the vessels in the kitchen, cleaning and getting things ready for the next morning, when she heard sounds from Mamayya's room. She went running to see if he was all right. Slowly opening the door, she looked inside to find him in a heap on the floor, sobbing uncontrollably. That was the first time she had seen him giving in to the disappointment in his son, the despair that he could not do anything for his wife, the loss of his life's companion, crying, giving in to his grief at their continuous travails. It was the picture of total and utter desolation. He was bent, bow-like, his shoulder blades sticking out, glasses on the floor, his head weighted down with all the disappointments. Radha sat next to him for a long time that night, not talking, just keeping him company. A slow anger against Prabhakar was building up inside her as she saw Mamayya sobbing and wiping his eyes. For the first time since Prabhakar's departure, Radha considered doing something to support the family. Perhaps she could find a job as a typist. She was sure that her typing and shorthand skills were still good.

Her own education had stopped immediately after high school. Although she wanted to go to college to get a Bachelor's degree, her father could not afford it. There were no decent colleges nearby, and if she had to go to a large township and stay in a hostel, there was no money. She had instead been encouraged to learn Sanskrit at home and go to a nearby typing school. She learnt typing and shorthand for six months. Not that she ever thought she would use these skills. A girl had to do something to keep herself occupied until her parents found the right man for her. At the typing school she discovered that Mrs. Bhanumathi, who helped her husband, Mr. Murthy, run the school, was an avid gardener. Instead of returning home immediately after classes, Radha would spend hours with Mrs. Bhanumathi in her garden, helping her tend to the flowers and the vegetable bed in the backyard. Mrs. Bhanumathi had a green thumb, and her plants flourished, their shoots growing aggressively, trying to reach for the sky, their leaves iridescent in all the different shades of green that only nature could generate. Mrs. Bhanumati showed Radha how to make compost from kitchen and garden waste and very effectively used the same compost in her garden. The flowers on the different plants bloomed profusely, almost feverishly, vying with each other in a soundless clash of colours. She handled every leaf, bud, flower and twig with tenderness, as though they were feeling entities. When she saw the peeping redness in nascent twigs or mango leaves, she would point these out to Radha, explaining that the skin of the leaf was so delicate that the sap shone through, or she would compare the delicate twigs to the arms and feet of a newborn. It was as though the plants were humans but fixed to the earth, unable to move. Mrs. Bhanumathi never went near the plants once darkness fell, saying that they were now asleep and ought not to be disturbed. It was a rule Radha followed in her nursery. Come nightfall, the plants were left alone and any more planting, trimming and arranging were done only the next morning.

It had been quite a while for the right match to come along, almost five years. With her parents' permission she took up a job as a typist. She got an award for being the best typist in the local firm she worked at. She started raising a small vegetable garden behind their decrepit home with its thatched roof. On those days that she was free, she would still visit Mrs Bhanumati, spending time with her in her garden and her backyard.

When Prabhakar's parents visited her parents and brought a proposal for Radha, her little family was delirious with joy. How often does a girl of her station get a husband like that—not to mention a family like that, with economic stability? That the groom's side had come on their own was considered a blessing. Even the expenses of the wedding, Mamayya had assured her parents, would be borne by him. Her parents had been simple folk. Her father and mother were both ailing at that time, and Radha readily and willingly agreed to the marriage so that both her parents would have peace of mind.

This evening, as she looked around her at the little pots of crotons with variegated leaves, cannas, hibiscus, yellow, white and red that stood inside along the wall on stone benches, encircling the main eating area, all of them from her nursery, she felt grateful that destiny had guided her otherwise and that circumstances had inspired her to start a nursery instead. Three months after Atthayya's passing away, the two younger children had suffered from a heat stroke in the middle of May with the peak summer reigning over them. Both Mukund and Sunanda had nearly died of dehydration. They frantically took the children to the nearby municipality clinic five miles away. Many years after this, Radha could still vividly recall their desperate rush to the clinic in an auto-rickshaw. Mamayya had Mukund on his lap and Radha held Sunanda. The children's bodies were hot and limp and their eyes glazed as they struggled to keep them open. Vasu sat at the front next to the driver. It was the longest five miles they had ever traveled. The auto driver recognized the gravity of the situation and how sick the children were and drove as fast as the three-wheeler let him, overtaking the buses and cars on the way, interminably honking and even eliciting the wrath of the people on the road. When they arrived at the clinic, Vasu jumped out even before the auto came to a stand still, to dash into the clinic and get help. Two nurses and a nurse's aide rushed out with wheel chairs and took Mukund and Sunanda inside. Suresh and Parvati had rushed to the clinic to be with them. During that week, while tending to the two young ones with the help of the nurses and Vasu, Radha's fighting spirit was ignited. She would be forever grateful for the kindness and compassion shown by perfect strangers to an old man, a harried, tired woman and her three young children. They had to start intravenous drips to replenish the fluids and the electrolytes, the doctor explained. The children's veins were collapsed due to the dehydration, their blood pressures low. While they were able to get Mukund's vein after a struggle, they had to do a cut down to get Sunanda's vein. Radha almost fainted when she saw the blood spurting from the ankle incision on Sunanda as the doctor exposed the vein and inserted the large bore needle. She had clung to the table in the corner by the dust-washed windows of the clinic, trembling, her entire being aching. Vasu held his mother, his arms around her, quiet, his eyes bright with unshed tears. That very night, they thought they had lost Sunanda. Her pulse had become weak and her heartbeat irregular. Dr. Ramakanth did not go home that night. He and the nurse started one more infusion after one more cut down, this time exposing the vein in the other foot. This time Radha stood stoic, prepared for the spurt of blood as the doctor exposed the vein. But the blood did not spill from the vein due to Sunanda's low blood pressure. They pumped more electrolytes into Sunanda throughout the night. By next morning, her heartbeat had returned to normal, her breathing was regular and she had bounced back by afternoon.

Dr. Ramakanth said he was going to keep both the children in the clinic for a few more days until they were out of danger and back to normal.

It was also the time they had very few savings, with the tomorrows looming like dark mountains on the fringe of an ocean of pecuniary uncertainty. The little seed of an idea for the nursery was sown late one night as she sat her vigil by the bedside of Mukund and Sunanda. Her soul had been given a fillip by the green tender coconuts brought by Dhananjay, a friend of Mamayya. She had always liked this name. *Dhananjay, one of the ten names bestowed on Arjun, the third Pandava Prince, the magnificent, immaculate warrior, fearless and bold... each name descriptive of his different attributes. Her father would sit her and her brother down when they were young and make them repeat all the ten names of Arjuna. Dhananjay meant the one who wins wealth. It was also the name of Lord Vishnu.* Dhananjay was tall and handsome and always well dressed, more often than not wearing business suits, with an air of unquestioned authority radiating from him. She could still remember the beaming face of Mamayya when the coconuts arrived.

"Coconut water restores some of the electrolytes," Dr. Ramakanth had said. That year in particular, coconuts had been expensive and quite simply unaffordable. Dhananjay visited them every day during that difficult week and had even arranged for a specialist from the city to come and see the children and give his expert opinion to Dr. Ramakanth. She asked Mamayya how he had come to know Dhananjay, and Mamayya told her that it was through some common friends. In a way she was glad that Dhananjay had entered their lives and grateful that he filled the void created by Prabhakar's absence in Mamayya's life. Dhananjay made it a point to visit them at least once a month. He lived in the city and seemed to have many business enterprises. Once in a while he brought his daughter, Lakshmi, and his niece Swarna with him. Both Lakshmi and Swarna were a year younger than Vasu, and Radha always felt happy when all the children played together. Once, Mamayya had mentioned that Dhananjay's was an extended family consisting of his two brothers and their wives and children and his elderly mother and father. Radha had wanted to ask Dhananjay about his wife, but then, thinking otherwise, checked herself. If he wanted to, he would bring up the topic of his wife himself. As a testimony to the tender green coconuts and the good they had done to her children, Radha chose the coconut palms as the first plants to be sold from her nursery. At the end of that week, she started growing her coconut palms. All the knowledge she had gained from Mrs. Bhanumati at the typing school now came into use.

She would always be thankful to Mrs. Bhanumati for inspiring and encouraging her to develop an interest in gardening. The first batch of coconut saplings, twenty of them, grew within a few weeks and she sold them at the local fair on a Tuesday evening. She had not realized how popular these plants were until people were clamoring for more. The next time she saw Dhananjay, Radha had thanked him profusely for all his help during the children's illness and for encouraging her to start her nursery. Over the years, Dhananjay also got her nursery many customers through his contacts in the business community.

This afternoon, as she waited, she relished the sight of the Cannas, which had grown well that year, with their bright yellow petals painted with red dots and stripes. The gossamer petals of the white, red and yellow hibiscus trembled in the light breeze flowing through the large windows. The clusters of lantanas, yellow, red and purple in the distance looked like colourful bouquets, hugging the fence. The trellises she had set up at the farthest corner of the garden—a garden that she had single handedly planned—to facilitate the growth of the creeper roses, were fully covered with green, white and red. She had suggested to Kamalnath that a fountain in the front of the restaurant would be a good idea. True to his nature, Kamalnath consulted his astrologer and, upon his recommendation, built a fountain not at the front but towards the side of the restaurant some distance from the mango tree, as per the dictates of *Vastu*. The front of the restaurant was left bare, and Radha then decided to build a rock garden there and hoped the astrologer would have no objections. The rock garden, with its white and red rocks interspersed with the colourful crotons and the hardy cactus plants, became the cynosure of eyes and very often visitors gathered in front of it and had their pictures taken. Around the restaurant building itself, hugging the stone wall, there were the jasmines in full bloom, the fragrance now carried over the back of a lazy zephyr. Even with the anxiety and disquiet inside her, she felt a sudden spurt of sheer pleasure at seeing these flourishing plants from her nursery. Many times, as she moved amidst the vast jungle of plants, creepers, trees in her large nursery, she had felt this exultation. Is this what the Creator experienced, she would think, this fulfillment and joy at the beauty and vastness of nature, the silent constant, cyclical renewal of the leaves, buds, flowers and fruits? The mysterious, even powerful, potential of a seed to grow into a gigantic tree—the knowledge of this power at times froze her while she was attending to her plants. Those singular moments of joy and achievement were worth all the pain and toil she had undergone in building up the nursery to what it was today: a local landmark and even a regular stop for the tourists. The nursery had become a place for botanical excursions, and batches of students from the local college came there in their college busses at least twice a year to get acquainted with the different plants. Sometimes the botany students would spend hours sketching the different plants with their leaves and flowers. In a way, the nursery had forced Radha to acquaint herself with botany—about annuals and perennials, fruit trees and vegetables, the different types of crotons and palm trees—to become a surrogate botany expert, making her comfortable with botanical terms. She hired an English tutor, Mr. Narayan, who came once a week and taught her to become fluent in the language. Four years after she started the nursery, she had gone to the city with her children to scour the shops for textbooks on botany. Along with learning botany, it became a necessity to arm herself with the knowledge of the different pests and insects that harmed the plants and trees and the proper measures to be taken against them. Her children and Parvati had helped her in this venture. Now, in their new home, there was a room dedicated to all the books they had acquired. Today, people from all walks of life consulted her about what plants to grow, when and where to place them in their gardens, when to water them and how much water was required by each plant. Once every six months, she would accompany the botany students around the nursery and teach. She had never thought that she would be a teacher one day, and it gave her great pleasure dispensing the knowledge gleaned over the years to these young students. An enterprise branching off from her efforts that had taken everyone by surprise, including her, had been the pickling and bottling business. One year, she had had such an abundant crop of tomatoes that she was left with the choice of gathering and selling the tomatoes or allowing them to become overripe and soft and fall to the ground, of no use to anyone. Instead, upon a sudden whim, she had gathered all the tomatoes and made a pickle from them, a grueling task entailing hours of standing in front of a large stove and stirring the tomato pulp. She had learnt making pickles from her mother, and now, after many years, she was putting that knowledge and skill to use. She had then bottled the pickle and sold it to some of the customers who had visited the nursery, little anticipating that they would demand more. The following year she did the same with the lemons and the mangoes. Then, Tony had arrived, and once she had trained him, he had made things a lot easier, taking up some of her responsibilities both in the nursery and at the pickle making station.

Waiting for Prabhakar, recollecting all their trials and tribulations, it suddenly dawned upon her that she should perhaps be thankful to him for having left them. But for his dereliction of his role as a husband, father and son, leaving them nearly destitute, she realized, she would always have been dependent on others and would not have become the independent and self-sufficient woman she was today. She would never have realized her own inner potential. Yes, she concluded, Prabhakar's departure and absence had turned out to be a blessing in disguise.

The peal of the temple bells startled her out of her reveries, and she looked up. From where she sat in the restaurant, the dome of the temple with its triangular flag was visible. As the sun slid from its zenith, its slanting rays caught the red tower of the temple, iridescent and imposing over the mountain. There was no road to the temple, just the thirty high steps. Once, Prabhakar, who was good with his geography and general knowledge, had sneered, saying, "Ha, they all call it the Hanuman Mountain when it's really a hill." He had a supercilious attitude and sniffed contemptuously as though outraged by people's inability to grasp the difference between a mountain and a hill. He seemed genuinely upset when an apparently educated man accompanied by his wife and small son had stopped at their place and asked for directions to the Hanuman Mountain. Radha had been serving snacks and coffee at that time. "I wonder if he has scabies?" she had thought to herself at that point, looking at the little boy scratching his hands and arms. He was wearing shorts reaching down to his knees. Parvathi had told Radha about the recent outbreak of scabies in the little municipality school she taught at. All the impoverished children of the neighbourhood went to this school. Parvathi had degrees in Science and education.

"Why are you so upset?" Radha later asked Prabhakar after the large man, his diminutive wife and scratching son had left. Prabhakar, the geography enthusiast, then gave a short lecture to her and Mamayya. He explained to them the concept of a mountain and a hill. He gave numbers, the height of a mountain in metres and feet. He mentioned words such as summit and topography and incline. Some of the details were lost on Radha, but Mamayya had smiled proudly at the knowledge dispensed by his son. The whole family had admired Prabhakar's ability to grasp scientific facts, numbers and statistics. He had been the brightest man she had encountered in her small orbit and had admired his intelligence and play with words, his wit. Prabhakar had had a felicity and fluency with not just English but three other languages. She would always feel inadequate and small before his intelligence and his accomplishments. At once, she would experience a twinge of guilt, as she did from time to time, that Prabhakar had married beneath him by acquiescing to his father's wishes, that she was not a match for him. As her children grew up, she began to feel that she must be educated at least for their sake and started reading whenever she had some spare time away from the nursery to increase her general knowledge. Over the years, Radha had read copiously about England and the United States and about the habits of the people living in those countries, the clothes they wore, the food they ate and the different climates prevailing in those regions.

A second letter from Prabhakar arrived two weeks ago, informing her that he was in India. Again, it was handwritten. This time, it had been two pages long. He wrote that he had to fly to Bangalore first on some business and from there would be visiting them. The letter was mostly about himself, his business and his plans of expanding it. There was no mention of the children. Just a token mention of his father, hoping that he was well. Radha wondered if Prabhakar even remembered the names of his children. Twenty-four hours ago, she had spoken to him on the phone. His voice was somehow thicker than what she remembered, his words slightly hesitant. Or maybe she had forgotten how his voice sounded after so many years, having had no verbal communication with him. He was staying in a hotel in the city, he told her. He said it accusatively, as though he was doing them a favor and that perhaps she should be thankful that he had not come over to the house and demanded his rightful place with them. Over the phone line, she could tell that he was taken aback when she mentioned the restaurant as the point of their rendezvous instead of their home.

"What is the name of that place again?" Prabhakar had asked, disbelief in his voice.

Radha repeated, "It is called "Hotel Highway Very Most Famous." At any other time, Prabhakar, the English enthusiast and now foreign-returned man, would have snorted or laughed and probably exclaimed, "What a name! Does anyone have respect for grammar or syntax anymore?" Radha was a little surprised that the peculiar name had not drawn forth this response from him. Several years after it opened, the name of the restaurant had indeed caused a lot of local unrest and loss of sleep for Kamalnath.

A busload of college students who had stopped at the restaurant for refreshments after a tiring day at a football tournament carried the news of this peculiar name to their college professors. Matters may very well have rested there, for most of the Professors of the college were old timers waiting to embrace retirement, peace and quiet with their generous pensions. But as such things have a way about them, even this was not to be. There was a Professor Seshadri, a young enthusiast of the English language, recently returned from England, who decided to take matters into his own hands. He made a list of the do's and don'ts about naming and syntax and sent it to one of the prominent local newspapers.

Point 1: It was a restaurant, not a hotel. Affixing the word "hotel" to a restaurant was an Indian habit—a funny Indian habit. A hotel was a place where people stayed for a night or two. A restaurant was a place where people came to eat. The word hotel needed to be scratched.

Point 2: The title should be either "Famous Highway Restaurant" or "Highway Restaurant." Moreover, it was so haughty, self-aggrandising, that this restaurant, sitting next to a highway, should so proclaim its non-existent fame and even attach the word "most." And whoever thought of adding "very" to "most"? Did people know anything about the use of superlatives? This was a brazen assault on the English language, the enraged Dr. Seshadri declared.

The debate about the restaurant was becoming quite acrimonious in the local newspapers. The newspaper that was pro-Dr. Seshadri, MA, PhD, wrote that, at last, here was a man who was trying to correct and polish the English of Indians and make them more respectable and presentable on the world stage. After all, everywhere you travelled in the world, people made fun of "Indian English." The other newspaper, which was pro-Kamalnath (the editor was a friend of Kamalnath, recipient of many free lunches and dinners at the restaurant), opined that the name was, after all, uniquely Indian, or *desi*. This newspaper further went on to argue that if the Westerners could come to our country and pronounce Indian names, distorting them in a discombobulated way, syllable by syllable, vowel by vowel, tearing into our "Sanskrit *Sandhis*," transforming them into unrecognizable gibberish with their tongues tied up in knots, then why on earth are the Indians being so fastidious about this imported language? After all, the pro-Kamalnath newspaper exhorted, English was only adopted due to its commercial advantage, its worldwide acceptance; if the English educated Indians became snobbish about it, they better be put in their place. Moreover, the paper went on to further enumerate, look at all the Indian words—guru, pundit, karma, nirvana, mantra and kismet, to name just a few—that had crept into or been borrowed by the English language. The newspaper war went on for a while. There was much back and forth with historical references and the names of the founding fathers and famous independence fighters of India, who were sadly no more, being dragged into the debate. There was the mention of Raja Ram Mohan Roy, Rabindranath Tagore and of course Gandhiji, Pandit Nehru and Sardar Patel. Anecdotal stories of the English spoken by the now departed beloved leaders were told with flourish. The beautiful English employed by the erudite Pandit Nehru in his book, *The Discovery of India,* which he wrote while in jail, was extolled, and the suggestion was made that perhaps Kamalnath and his ilk and people like him should read this book by Nehru to understand the beauty and glory of English. The local sales of *The Discovery of India* went up and prompted Mukund, an avid reader, to go and purchase a volume. The story that Pandit Nehru wrote his famous book while imprisoned prompted another newspaper article on all the books that were written by Indian political leaders and world leaders while in prison. The words Anglophiles and Anglophobes were bandied about. The question then was raised about which past and departed leaders had been Anglophobes and which leaders had been Anglophiles. The etymology of the words "phile" and "phobe" was discussed. The name of the restaurant had unwittingly become a gold mine for wit, humour, penmanship and rancor, of lessons in etymology and awakening the curiosity of the younger Indians about the Independence movement, for resurfacing of the literature birthed during the imprisonment of the different leaders and of awakening festering enmities between the editors of the two newspapers. A local gossip magazine then published a story regarding the two warring editors, about their longstanding friendship, and how their falling in love with the same young woman had fractured it. The magazine did not reveal which editor had won the hand of the young woman. In response to this gossip, both editors vehemently denied the story in their respective newspapers.

The very energetic and ebullient Dr. Seshadri, MA, PhD, clearly an Anglophile, even headed a small demonstration one strategic Sunday when the restaurant was packed with customers. Radha had gone to the restaurant to deliver some plants with her helper and to discuss with Kamalnath as to the best place in the large garden to plant them. The young professor and about twenty of his ardent followers came in a bus. They wore jeans and T-shirts that were emblazoned with quotes from GB Shaw, Oscar Wilde and Shakespeare. A pretty young girl, confident in her stride and purpose, her thick, long hair flowing behind her, held up a banner that screamed: "Please respect the English Language." The back of her T-shirt, dark green in colour, had a quote from Oscar Wilde in stark contrasting white letters. Radha, who had been close enough to the young woman, stared at her across the fence, admiring her stance, and as she moved away, her eyes fell upon the quotation on her T-shirt: "To lose one parent may be regarded as a misfortune, to lose both looks like carelessness," and had mentally made a note to ask Mukund from which one of Oscar Wilde's plays this quotation was. A young bearded man, his hair unkempt, wearing a red T-shirt with a GB Shaw quotation, held up a banner that declared, "Language reflects culture." One banner chided Kamalnath openly for using the word "hotel": "Do you know the difference between a hotel and a restaurant, Mr. Kamalnath?" Another banner had the preferred names for the restaurant: "Highway Restaurant,"

"Famous Restaurant," and even "Kamalnath Restaurant." A large banner questioned, "What is 'most' famous about this eatery, Mr. Kamalnath?" There was one banner condemning the use of "very" with the superlative "most." "Very, most impertinent use of the English Language," the banner screamed. Kamalnath was mollified at the banners being paraded and the slogans being hurled at him and the restaurant, and was beginning to see the end of his enterprise in his every waking minute. He was not an uneducated person as this whole affair was purporting him to be. He was a "BA Pass, second class," as he had once told Mamayya. That evening, with the banners and all the noise in front of the main gate, the flustered Kamalnath, lacking the courage to come face to face with the protestors, asked Radha to meet him at the back of the restaurant and came out through the kitchen door that opened on to the large backyard, where there was the vegetable garden. The ripe red tomatoes dominated almost half the vegetable bed. The eggplants, with healthy gleaming purple skins, were ready to be picked. The green chilies hung in clusters. The lemon and guava trees were flourishing. The plantain trees at the perimeter of the backyard were lush and green with a few of them bowed down by the weight of the plantains. After her discussion with Kamalnath regarding where to plant the okra saplings she had brought from her nursery, Radha had left, assuring him that the furor over the restaurant's name will soon subside.

Kamalnath bore the insults hurled at him and his business with great fortitude. The restaurant guests luckily did not seem to be affected by this fight over the English language raging outside, and were enjoying the tasty food served up by Malathi and the waiters, being only mildly amused at the sideshow put on by the students with their banners. The demonstrators left after an hour. Kamalnath and his employees heaved a sigh of relief. Kamalnath, more determined than ever, amplified his efforts at appeasing Lord Hanuman. With redoubled vigor, he brought a five-foot statue of the God and placed it in the centre of the restaurant. The previous day, he had workers build a small pedestal to accommodate the God. He surrounded the idol with potted plants from the nursery. The blooming red hibiscus formed a ring of fire around the idol. An unexpected result, which gave Kamalnath great pleasure, was the fervor with which the customers paid respects to the idol in the restaurant. Most of them were devotees who came for refreshments after their visit to the Hanuman temple. It was as though they could not get enough of the grace of this God. His superhuman deeds so seemed to fill their minds.

Then, at the end of June, a severe thunderstorm struck. It drenched the entire area for miles. The water lines broke, power lines fell from the weight of fallen trees and the large cloth banner proclaiming "Hotel Highway Very Most Famous" became drenched and limp and lifeless. The two poles holding the banner keeled over one night, and the hotel became temporarily nameless. The storm was a boon of sorts as the hostels, the local University and colleges closed due to the broken power and water lines and everyone who could go somewhere left, including the temperamental Professor Seshadri. Two weeks later, when everything had dried up, the emboldened Kamalnath put up a large aluminum board with the name of the restaurant in red, green and blue paint outside the double gates leading to the garden and the restaurant, with much fanfare and religious chanting. The satin banner with the name was placed at the archway entrance of the restaurant. Lord Hanuman, Kamalnath firmly believed, had sent the storm and had inimitably, in his own way, taken care of the problem. The linguistic and syntactical furor was forgotten. When Professor Seshadri returned after four weeks, he had much bigger fish to fry than waging a war on a wayside restaurant with its swaggering banner. He had, of course, quite tempestuously entered into a linguistic argument over certain Indian English terms in the newspapers. Nobody broached the topic of the restaurant's name again, and Kamalnath felt strangely vindicated.

In the distance, Radha could see the tail lights of vehicles hugging the acclivity of the road. The hairpin bends became sharper and steeper, with the mountains merging into one another like the undulating folds of a thick garment. On the highway, the busses and the lorries rumbled incessantly like some restless beasts, and the smaller vehicles sounded like bees as the engines revved up to climb the slope. The cloth banner at the arch of the restaurant entrance, with its fringe of rich, thick yellow threads now fluttered in the breeze, and the bright red and blue words danced over the archway. "Most Famous": the words showed the scale of ambition of the owner.

"There is nothing wrong in being ambitious, Radha." That is what he, Prabhakar, had told her sixteen years ago. The way he said it seemed as though he was admonishing her for even questioning his ambition. He had told her he was leaving the country. There was no mention of his final destination, no mention of when he would return. He had packed his bags and left. She had watched wordlessly. Prabhakar never hugged his children, never turned back as he got into the taxi, not even once, to wave goodbye to the three of them, as they clung to their mother. For many months, Radha hated the word "ambition." It had become a vulgar word, a word that wrought havoc on families, on human beings. If ambition meant leaving your wife behind, your children behind, breaking all past ties, even with one's own parents, she did not want to have any of it. If she had the power and wherewithal, she would erase that word "ambition" from the dictionary and common parlance. It was a deadly word, like a strange infectious creature, like a disease spreading virus. She waited at the table, looking at her watch, trying to stop her heart from racing, remembering Mamayya's cautions and injunctions.

"Do not start the conversation first," Mamayya had told her. "Let him do all the talking." Radha had nodded.

"Please do not invite him to the house. I cannot think of bonding with that man," this from Mukund.

"Amma, what do you really want to do?" This from Sunanda. "Do you want him here in this house, living under the same roof after all these years? I cannot even imagine sharing my meals with him."

"Why can't you all go with me and each one of you can express your true feelings there in front of him," said Radha. There were immediate protests from all of them. No, they wanted to leave it to her, this decision.

"Use your heart, Amma, not your intellect." This from Vasu. Mamayya nodded vigorously.

She was trying ineffectively to read the local Telugu magazine she had brought with her. The name of the magazine was "Neti Vanita, ["Today's Woman,"]. The magazine was very popular in their large town and the city, for unctuously giving all sorts of advice to women. In gratitude for allowing the magazine to run an entire article in one of their issues about her nursery, the magazine staff sent her all their issues for free for one year. She had named her nursery "Sahana": endurance, a testament to what she and her family had endured over the years and to the spirit of survival in her, Mamayya and the children. The title the editor had chosen for the article had been "Radha's Sahana," personalising it a bit, giving it a dramatic twist, but people had loved the article, and it had helped to promote more visitors and customers. The centerspread in the magazine showed the profusion of flowers in the pots arranged in tiers in her nursery and the serendipitous presence of two large butterflies hovering above the flowers. Radha had removed the centerspread and framed it. In the current issue of the same magazine she had brought with her to the restaurant, there was an article about unfaithful spouses; what a coincidence, thought Radha. "Why are men unfaithful?" That was the headline of the article. There was a photo, a black and white one, depicting a teary-eyed woman watching a man as he walked away.

A few minutes later, Lakshman brought her a glass of lemonade. She smiled at Lakshman as she took the proffered glass and then asked him if he could go and find out if Tony wanted something to drink. Laksman nodded, went and returned saying he could not find Tony or the car. Radha was surprised that Tony had left without telling her and then she remembered his mentioning something about the car running out of petrol. Perhaps he had gone to get some petrol. She scanned over the rim of the glass in her hand, and saw the trickle of people entering the restaurant. Scouring the road for Prabhakar had become her pastime during the first few months after he had left. Any sound of a distant car, any man with a similar build would make her heart beat in anticipation. Her eyes, seeking a returning Prabhakar, had enslaved themselves to false hopes. For a few years, the question or doubt of her forgiving him for "that other woman" did not cross her mind. He was, after all, her children's father, and absolutely essential for the reconstitution of her broken family. Radha looked back upon that time and wondered when exactly it was that she had given up on his ever returning. It had not happened in a single moment or a day. She came back to the magazine article. It was so stale, this story of deserting, unfaithful husbands. Over the years, the social environment had changed, and there were now emerging a few unfaithful women as well. What are the early signs of unfaithfulness, of evolving adultery? Early signs—like a disease. "Signs and symptoms" was a terminology she had become familiar with ever since Vasu had begun medical college. In the US, Sunanda once told her, a college is called a school. At the beginning, Radha blamed herself for Prabhakar deserting them. She had failed to see the warning signs. How could she have missed them? One day she had gone out with Prabhakar to shop for clothes before Diwali. It was perhaps the second or third time that she and Prabhakar had gone out as a couple since their wedding. They were at one of the more expensive shops in the city when they ran into a friend of Prabhakar. He had come in an imported car, quite a rarity in those days, with his wife, a very sophisticated woman. Radha had secretly admired the poise of this woman, with her well-done hair, her blemish-free hands and red nail polish. Prabhakar was very jovial with his friend and his wife, accompanying them to their car and watching them drive away, staring after the car until it had turned the corner. When he returned to pay at the counter for their purchases, he had a faraway look in his eyes. On the return home on the scooter, he seemed to resent her hand as she placed it on his shoulder while riding on the pillion. Six months later, he had left. Yes: she, Radha, had so missed all the signs. She had failed to keep up to the standards desired by him. She recounted that day and wondered if the sophisticated woman they had met in the shop had reminded Prabhakar of Leena and whether this event was what triggered his leaving. She had been afraid that, one day, even her children might recognise the same deficiencies in her and may come to treat her in disdain. Surprisingly, that never happened. In fact, the three of them had showered her with so much love and devotion that once in a while she would catch her breath with gratitude. In a gradual process made subtle by the passage of time, the children had become hers. The concept of "our children," which she embraced in the "Prabhakar days," had evaporated due to his absence.

Radha turned around and looked at the fountain. The light breeze was spraying the water from the fountain, and droplets were collecting over the rose plants placed around it. A little behind the fountain was the mango tree that had arrived as a sapling from her nursery. In the early years, Radha would herself go to the different houses or businesses, taking the plants with her, helping her customers decide the best place in their gardens or backyards where they could be planted. She realized with dismay that many of her customers were quite ignorant of the immense potential of growth in these saplings. She still remembered with some amusement the bewildered look on Kamalnath's countenance as she picked a large clearing for the mango sapling, deftly planting it and arranging triangular brick pieces around the plant and then placing a little wicker wall around it "to protect it from strong winds and from a goat or sheep that may stray from a villager's herd," she had explained. And yes, that generous clearing was necessary around this sapling because it would grow into a tree. Years later, the strong trunk of the mango tree, its sturdy branches and the bunches of mangoes hanging from them evoked a sense of pride and gratitude in her.

She looked up again to scan the new visitors, searching for Prabhakar. Her attention was drawn to the makeshift dais that had been made for the occasion of Lord Hanuman's birthday. The dais was six by six feet and had red and green cloth covering the sides. Close to fifty chairs were placed in front of the dais. There were buntings hanging from the bright yellow canopy, and a few "Lord Hanuman" clones were gathering around the dais. Some of them had their bodies painted blue, with red vermilion paint around their eyes and lips. Others had red paint on their entire body and face. Around their waists they wore a *dhoti* tucked between the legs, the *dhoti* riding high above the knees. They wore garlands of hibiscus, basil leaves and marigolds that covered their chests. Wide decorated belts girded their waists from which tails hung, like Lord Hanuman's. There were excited shouts as a bus stopped and discharged another thirty or more "Hanuman clones."

Lakshman brought her a plate of snacks and asked whether he could get her some coffee. "Today is Hanuman Jayanthi," Lakshman told her happily. "We are expecting a record number of people." In the restaurant, extra folding tables were being opened and arranged, spilling over into the garden. Radha tried to relax a little, not to show her anxiety and sat back, wondering what demands Prabhakar was going to make. Would he have the decency to apologise for his desertion of them sixteen years ago? The first few years, she had carefully preserved his clothes, books and papers, even the checkbooks pertaining to his closed bank account, with the hope that he would return. Five summers post-Prabhakar, there was a charity drive in the local college—students were collecting old clothes, old utensils for a village they had adopted. Mamayya decided to give away all of Prabhakar's clothes. As was his custom, he did ask Radha for her permission. If a father wanted to give away his offspring's clothes, did she have the right to say no? As she had watched him empty the large Godrej cupboard, it suddenly dawned on Radha that Prabhakar had accumulated more clothes than she and the children put together. That he had been a vain man occurred to her, then, as Mamayya removed shirt after shirt, trousers, safari suits and a multitude of socks and shoes and collected them in four large bags. She had asked Mamayya, "Do you want to ask Suresh if he would like to use some of these clothes? They both are nearly the same size and some of them are new."

"No, let us give these away. They are occupying too much room here and you can put your clothes in the cupboard instead," Mamayya had answered. Probably realising that he had been unnecessarily abrupt with her, he smiled and said, "Do you really think Suresh would wear these clothes? He dresses more sensibly." She saw a vehemence and anger with which he handled his son's clothes—a certitude—that with the giving up of his son's clothes, he was in a way giving up the memories and ties that bound them. A year later, some of the books followed the same route to a local upcoming library. Prabhakar's slanting tall writing was there on every single book—Prabhakar Kumar. Prabhakar never used his family name because he had thought it too gauche, too rustic, as he had once told her. Finally, the only artifact she was able to save was the broken wooden plaque with Prabhakar's name on it. Mamayya saw the broken plaque as he was emptying the cupboard of its clothes and had said nothing to Radha about it. He had removed some of the pictures of Prabhakar from the walls of the house. Taking a cue, Radha had removed the large framed wedding photograph of her with Prabhakar that stood on the dresser in the bedroom. She then replaced it with photographs of Mamayya, Atthayya and herself with the children.

# Shanta

Shanta, who had been busy lighting lamps around the Hanuman idol in the restaurant approached Radha, a radiant smile upon her face. She was a very beautiful woman, tall, lean, with an effulgent personality, thick dark hair flowing down to her hips, and this afternoon she was resplendent in a red silk saree, the vermillion dot upon her forehead, larger than on most days, a tuberose garland around her neck, jasmines adorning her hair. Her face was iridescent, her large eyes bright and Kohl lined, her perfect lips enhanced by the red lipstick she wore. She does look like a goddess, thought Radha. At the time of the furor over the restaurant's name, when Kamalnath put up the statue of Lord Hanuman in the restaurant, Shanta began to light little oil lamps around the deity and decorate the deity with strings of jasmines and other flowers grown around her home.

Shanta's father had been one of the first priests to serve in the Hanuman temple. She was the youngest of five siblings: three brothers and two sisters. The oldest, Shanta's sister, had married when Shanta was still very young, the three brothers marrying later and finding jobs in the city. None of the brothers had shown any interest in the priesthood, deeply disappointing Shanta's father. What really caused her father's heartbreak though, was

Shanta returning home after she had been banished from her husband's house. Her three miscarriages and her own depression following these had all led to her being subjected to mental and physical abuse and treated as an outcast by her husband's family. Her husband was making plans to marry again, so she had returned to her parents' house. Her father had been ailing for some time, unable to carry on his priestly duties. Her mother who had always been feeble was not doing well either. Shanta took it upon herself to care for her parents, taking them to the doctors when necessary. The three brothers did not contribute to the care of the parents and stayed away, afraid to get involved. Shanta's sister had died several years ago and was survived by her son and daughter. Both Shanta's parents died within seven years of her return. They left their house for her, aware that it was her only refuge. There was a small extension of the house that could be rented, and Shanta lived off the rent.

Kamalnath, who had previously shunned Shanta as a potential threat to his business, fearing that the presence of a woman who behaved strangely would keep the customers away, had a transformation which was in no small part attributable to his own experience of being the object of ridicule due to the restaurant's idiosyncratic name. Shanta could come and eat in the restaurant for free anytime she wanted, Kamalnath declared, and she could mingle with the patrons if she so desired.

Around this time, a rumour began as a small whisper that Shanta was a reincarnation of Anjana Devi, the mother of Lord Hanuman. Over time, the whisper turned into a full-throated cry that metamorphosed into a certainty. Shanta was now a local celebrity. People began to shower her with gifts and money. Shanta's brothers tried to possess the house she lived in and hired a lawyer, and she was on the verge of being rendered homeless. Luckily, Mamayya and Dhananjay, who got wind of it, got a prominent lawyer, also an ardent devotee of Lord Hanuman, to represent her in the court and fight for her. The law ruled in favour of Shanta. Relatives who had broken their ties with her suddenly wanted to renew them as she, in their eyes, emerged as an interesting and even limitless source of income. Shanta's nephew, her sister's son and his wife, who had always helped and supported her, came to her aid. They were now managing her affairs. It was also rumoured that she was on a new medication prescribed by an eminent "mind doctor" in the city and that she was slowly beginning to be normal. Having been a witness to this entire saga, Radha was convinced that it was not Shanta who was mad but the world around her. All she had seen in Shanta was a woman who had been wronged by her husband and his family, later by her own brothers and by society at large, and who had craved affection and friendship. Society, Radha realized, does not give women too many second chances. While men like Shanta's husband remarry blithely, a woman like Shanta remarrying was a rare entity, largely due to the prevailing societal taboos and restrictions.

Since her return to the parental home, Shanta had kept herself busy, reading all the existing literature on Lord Hanuman, and today she was considered an expert not only on the divinity and immense powers of Lord Hanuman but also on the *Sundara Kanda*, the fifth book of the Ramayana depicting the journey of Hanuman to Sri Lanka as Lord Rama's messenger and his deeds there, including his meeting with Sita Devi, Lord Rama's wife. Shanta had once told her:

*Lord Hanuman was a child prodigy in the acquisition of all his superhuman powers. Mythology had it that, due to a curse by one of the* rishis, *Hanuman forgot all the powers acquired by him. However, when the occasion arose and he was reminded about his innate powers, he was able to resurrect and activate them to help and protect others.*

One summer morning, three years after starting her nursery, when Radha had gone to the restaurant to take care of some newly potted plants and check on them, Shanta walked up to her and, addressing her as *Akka* (sister), gave her the offerings from the temple, flavoured rice and fruits, insisting that Radha eat them then and there. Radha then remembered how rude and insensitive Prabhakar had been on the steps of the temple a few years ago and wondered if Shanta remembered that incident or had forgotten about it. After Radha ate the rice, Shanta, appeased, began to follow her around the garden, helping her and carrying the water for the plants. She would do this every time Radha went to the restaurant, talking to her about the children she could never have and her nephew and his wife who cared for her. A friendship developed between them, and once in a while, when Radha sat down to have her tea or lunch at the restaurant after a morning of work and replanting in the garden, she would ask Shanta to join her. There was something child-like and naïve about Shanta that was very appealing. Radha was grateful to Shanta for not bringing up the subject of Prabhakar. Over the years, they developed a strong bond and friendship. Many times, Shanta had visited them at their home and Radha always enjoyed taking her around the nursery.

This evening, Shanta embraced Radha and told her happily about all the arrangements in preparation for the Hanuman Jayanti. When Radha invited her to have some coffee and snacks with her, she refused, saying she was fasting. Shanta asked Radha to stay back for a while to hear her speech on Lord Hanuman and the importance of the Sundara Kanda.

"Akka, our stories are similar to Lord Hanuman's story. We both did not know of our own capabilities, until life forced us to recognise and renew our own inner strength. I will see you soon, Akka." Saying this, Shanta bounded towards the dais and started talking animatedly with the Hanuman clones who had been waiting for her, blessing those who touched her feet in reverence. She seemed to have effortlessly accepted this mantle of being Lord Hanuman's reincarnated mother without embarrassment or self-consciousness. In fact, she seemed to take a childish pleasure in this role.

Radha looked up as a black car drove up to the front of the restaurant. Two women in brightly patterned dresses got out. As they approached the restaurant laughing and talking, she could see their matching handbags, each a red and black flattened box slung crosswise. Along with them there was an older man and two children. Prabhakar would be coming alone, she thought, and went back to the magazine she had brought with her. She looked at her watch—an Indian made one, gifted by her children. She insisted on buying only Indian. Today she could afford very costly goods, including foreign made perfumes, jewelry, and watches. But she bought only Indian-made goods as far as possible. It was as though Prabhakar deserting her and the children for foreign shores had roused the patriotism lying dormant within her. "Buy Indian, Be Indian," the Indian politicians always exhorted, a slogan also carried on some of the city and tourist busses. She, Radha, carried this slogan in her heart. She had put off acquiring many of the luxuries of modern life as she was afraid to succumb to materialism.

"It was not materialism anymore but being just practical—to own a refrigerator, a TV, a modern gas stove and a car," her children convinced her.

As she sat waiting, Radha remembered the horoscope for the day. On any other day, she would have ignored the daily horoscope in the newspaper. But today, she had read it with great anticipation and trepidation. *"A friend is going to come clean about a long-held secret. This meeting could turn your life upside down."* Radha reflected on the prediction and wondered if Kamalnath or Malathi or Shanta had something interesting to reveal.

# Dhananjay

"Hello, Radha," the familiar voice surprised her. She looked up and saw Dhananjay smiling down at her.

"Dhananjay, what brings you here at this hour?"

"Well, you and Prabhakar."

"What? Do you know Prabhakar? Are you friends and you never told me all these years?" Radha asked, surprised. She thought of the horoscope and its prediction.

"Hahaha. Friend is not a word I would use to describe my relationship with Prabhakar."

"Stop the suspense and do not give me any more anxiety than what I already have," Radha replied, almost chiding him. He was an old friend of the family, after all, and she could take certain liberties with him. They had become even closer after Vasu started his medical college because Lakshmi and Swarna, Dhananjay's daughter and niece, were Vasu's classmates and they were all going to graduate together once their internships were over. While still in medical school, both the girls and other classmates of Vasu would get together at the house before their exams, discussing and debating the likely questions that could come up in the tests. It always gave Radha great pleasure to see these young people so intense with their studies, and she would have plenty of food prepared for them as they ploughed through their different books. Radha had also observed a certain closeness of Vasu with Swarna and had wondered if there was a budding romance between them. Swarna was Dhananjay's sister's daughter and Radha loved both Lakshmi and Swarna, as they were always thoughtful and considerate about others, much like Dhananjay himself.

"No Radha," Dhananjay replied. "I am here to support you, to give you the moral courage you need to confront Prabhakar. You will be happy to know that I have also convinced Mamayya to join us. Tony has gone to pick him up."

"Thank you, Dhananjay."

"I have waited a long time to tell you my side of the story, Radha."

Puzzled, Radha watched him quietly as he took out an object from his jacket pocket. As he laid it on the table, she could not believe her eyes. She stared at the missing half of the wooden plaque with the word "Leena" embossed on it. The same colour and texture of wood. The same red and green undulating border. There were small leaves around the letters, just as they were with the portion of the plaque she had so carefully preserved. "Leena"—the letters were tall and bold in nice calligraphy, the "L" rounded at the ends, the "e"s, the "n" sloping and slanting and the "a" dauntingly curvaceous. As beautiful as Leena perhaps, she thought.

She had often wondered why she retained the half plaque she had discovered in the cupboard and could not come up with a proper answer. Did she keep it as a reminder of Prabhakar's perfidy or was she keeping it as a remembrance of him, or did she like the pain it evoked? Maybe, even, as a last vestige of proof that he had once lived with them.

"I am the other half of your story, Radha. You see, I am Leena's husband, rather, ex-husband," Dhananjay said simply, sitting down in front of her, the chair groaning under his weight. This abrupt utterance, with no flair, no drama, was so shocking that Radha's mouth fell open, her hand rising to her neck and then slowly to her mouth. A hundred thoughts raced through her mind, a thousand unspoken words lay dormant waiting to erupt in a volcano of questions. All the images of Leena she had carried these many years came back to life. With the passage of time, Leena's beauty, charm and enchantment had only increased in Radha's imagination. She saw a tall, lithe beauty, intelligent, educated, cultured, and a woman that any man would be proud to be seen with. She had realized with recurrent pain after he had left that Prabhakar had never asked her, his wife, to accompany him anywhere, especially to places where they would have encountered his colleagues or old classmates. Now, confronted by Dhananjay, Radha mentally chided herself for being so short sighted, so caught up in her own side of the story that she had never in all these years thought about or even imagined, how her husband, absconding with Leena, could have impacted another family or other lives. More was the wonder that this man, the very embodiment of confidence and strength, sitting in front of her, had suffered the same fate as her. She imagined Dhananjay and Leena together. They must_have made a beautiful couple, unlike the odd couple she and Prabhakar made, with Prabhakar far better looking than herself.

"Yes," Dhananjay reiterated, "I am Leena's ex-husband." He continued: "Mamayya told me that he had tried to dissuade you from meeting Prabhakar, even acknowledging his letter. He suspects that you are doing all this for him, because Prabhakar is his son; or you are doing this for the children. The truth is that Mamayya does not care for him and does not want him back. He wanted you to make this decision, about letting Prabhakar back or not, on your own." She wondered if she was that transparent. Were her intentions not honourable? Two days ago, she had sat in front of her mirror, confronting herself in it. Through that mirror, she tried to look into her own heart. Did she really want Prabhakar back in her life? Was she doing this in part for Mamayya? Despite his anger against Prabhakar, despite his warnings to her, wouldn't any father want his son back in the fold? She felt like that sparrow again, before the inevitable thunderbolt struck, yet there was no darkness and gloom this time. That sparrow had grown, and there was the light of success and achievement around her. In her hand was the power to catch that thunderbolt and stop its force and destruction. She had tried to build a secure, loving family once, only to have it wounded and truncated. Mamayya and she had restored that family to its original strength sans Prabhakar. The children had done surprisingly well without their father and she had almost single handedly built the largest nursery in that region, no small achievement for a woman like her with practically no money and resources to begin with. Her only wealth, only strength, lay in the support of Mamayya, her children, the support of Suresh and Parvathi and the friendship of Dhananjay. Would Prabhakar come back into their lives only to destroy everything again, including her own confidence and self-assurance? Like the thunderbolt?

Dhananjay continued with his story:

*Leena took off on a Sunday morning, leaving me and our daughter Lakshmi. She did not tell me, Lakshmi or the housekeeper,*

*Manasi. I had gone for my morning run and by the time I returned an hour later, Leena was nowhere to be found and a couple of suitcases were missing. Lakshmi was still sound asleep in her room. Initially, I was under the impression that Leena had gone to Mumbai in a huff to be with her father. We were always having fights and intense disagreements over the most trivial of things. We were just very incompatible, with neither of us willing to give in to the other. I tried to compromise and adjust in the beginning, believe me, because I wanted the marriage to work. But a unilateral effort never works in a marriage. When I called her father in Mumbai a day later, he came out with the whole sordid story—the college crush turning into a steadfast attraction. His voice trembling and apologetic, the old man related the saga, it even surpassed the most brazen themes of filmdom, and he told me that Leena was now with Prabhakar in London. He hung up, apologising and sobbing, even offering to raise Lakshmi if she became a burden to me as a single father. I told him firmly and without any hesitation that I was going to file for a divorce and that if at any time Leena tried to take away Lakshmi from me, she would be facing a very long and arduous legal battle. The funny thing is that Prabhakar had attended our wedding and I had met him. He brought a gift, a music box. Leena was very fond of collecting music boxes. This half of the plaque I only discovered after Leena left.* At this juncture, Radha interrupted him.

"Who married first? Was it Prabhakar or Leena?"

Dhananjay was a little taken aback, a puzzled look on his face, as to the relevance of this question.

"Leena and I married first," he replied. "You see, we were engaged when we were quite young. Leena was fifteen and I was seventeen. This was the wish of the grandparents from both sides. Our grandfathers had been business partners. The engagement ceremony itself was performed with a lot of pomp in Mumbai with a host of guests attending. As we grew up I think both Leena and I realized that we were not really compatible. But, to keep the promise from both sides we went ahead with the wedding. I did not even get a hint from Leena about her affair with Prabhakar." So, thought Radha, it had been Leena who had married first, not Prabhakar. And Prabhakar had probably bowed to the pressure from his parents. She was not sure if she got any solace from knowing that Leena had married first.

"Prabhakar and you, from what I heard, married two years later." Dhananjay said and continued his narrative:

*There was a friend and colleague of Prabhakar who gave me details regarding your family. I got your address from him. The most difficult part was setting up a meeting with Mamayya. How do you confront an elderly man whose son had left him, his sick wife, his three grandchildren and their mother? And you? You who I had never known, or met—what words of comfort do I have to say to a young wife? For some odd reason, I felt guilty and responsible for Leena's absconding with Prabhakar. Could I have changed the tide of events? I do not know. It took me three whole days and several cups of coffee to write a letter to Mamayya. I was so grateful when I received a simple postcard from him setting up a meeting place and time. At our first meeting, he held my hands, not letting go, an elderly man, bent over with this terrible burden, weeping openly. I was angry, furious, with Prabhakar, with Leena, our tangled fates. I cursed the day that I had married Leena. A slow realization dawned upon me that whatever action that had to be taken would have to be by me. I recall Mamayya's exact words as he narrated your condition to me. He said, "My Radha is like a broken doll; she will not recover. I cannot repair the damage that has been caused. I have done a great injustice to my*

*Radha." I realized then that, for him, you meant a lot more than his own son. I tried to convince him that perhaps you should file a police complaint and at least get a court order that Prabhakar should pay child support. I had contacts and would be able to help him, I said. But he refused to do that. From that day onwards, as you are aware, we have met regularly, like two old cronies. Yes, it is a very strange friendship I have with Mamayya and all of you. I wanted to tell you the first time I met you about my relationship with Leena, but that was the time when both Mukund and Sunanda were ill and you had brought them to the clinic. Later when I did want to tell you, Mamayya dissuaded me and I felt that you may not feel comfortable with me once you knew the truth. But I hope you can accept my friendship in spite of knowing what you do now.*

Radha was still digesting all the information given by Dhananjay when she saw Mamayya walking towards their table. She looked at her watch again and exclaimed, "Prabhakar should be here any minute now. I am glad Mamayya and you are both here."

Dhananjay seemed somewhat relieved as he got up to greet Mamayya.

"I see that you have told your half of the story to Radha," Mamayya commented, pointing to the wooden plaque.

"Yes, he did," Radha answered. "I am still in shock by this revelation."

"Sorry, Radha. I hope you are not angry with me, that after all these years, I chose today of all days to tell you my story."

"No, Dhananjay, I am not angry. I was so blinded by my own side of this saga that it had never occurred to me all this time that Leena could have a family of her own and that her family may have suffered the same way we did. I am also shocked that she could leave her child behind. Was it tough to raise your daughter on your own? Did Lakshmi miss her mother?"

"Lakshmi was distraught for the first two weeks, always crying for her mother, not wanting to go to school and not wanting to eat. Luckily, my parents rushed to my aid within three days, and then my brothers and their wives decided that we should all live together as a joint family, and they moved in with me within a few months. That was a welcome relief. My brothers' wives have been so kind and loving and have doted upon Lakshmi so much that she has come out of whatever trauma she has experienced. I owe them so much. Also, the arrival of my brothers' children, her cousins, was very therapeutic for Lakshmi. Things became really good and almost normal after that."

"Does Lakshmi know the truth?"

"She does now. Immediately after Leena left, I told Lakshmi that her mother had gone on a business trip and had an accident and had died. It was a terrible lie, and I felt badly about it. Lakshmi was only eight years old. When she turned fourteen, I sat her down and told her the truth."

"How did she take it?"

"She did not speak to me for a whole week. At the end of the week, though, I do not know how it happened—maybe my mother with whom Lakshmi is very close, had something to do with it—but Lakshmi came to me on her own and started talking. I was in my study one day and she crept up on me and hugged me. She thanked me for being both a mother and a father to her and said she was very sorry she had reacted the way she did when I had told her the truth. She expressed her gratitude that everyone, especially her two aunts, had showered her with so much love."

Dhananjay continued, "Lakshmi used to have a picture of her mother by her bed side all these years. But after she learnt the truth, she removed that picture and I did not ask her about it."

"There is something else I wanted both you and Mamayya to know."

"Oh, Dhananjay, are you going to give us some more shocking news?" Radha asked.

"Well, it is something you and Mamayya should know because it may influence the way you view Prabhakar, the way this meeting may go."

Radha's heart sank. She did not want Mamayya to be subjected to any more unpleasantness about his son.

"Tell us everything," Mamayya said. "At this point, nothing about Prabhakar will shock me."

With some hesitation, Dhananjay said, "Leena and Prabhakar visited India six years after they married in London. They came to Mumbai to visit her father and show him their sons. They spent a whole month in India."

Mamayya sat still, his expression stoic. Finally, he spoke, "I don't expect anything better from my cowardly son. He did not have the decency or courage to tell me he was leaving in the first place."

"How did you know about this visit?" Radha asked.

"Because Leena called me."

"What?"

"Yes, she called me—brazen of her, right? She wanted to talk to Lakshmi. I never revealed this even to you, Mamayya. There was no point. If Prabhakar had wanted, he could have called you, his father, at least, but he didn't. And if he had called, you would have told me."

"Did she talk to Lakshmi?"

"Lakshmi was fourteen and I had already told her the truth. Fortunately, at that time, she was away in Malaysia on a holiday with my brothers and their families. It was a treat for her fourteenth birthday, which both my sisters-in-law had planned for a while. I could not go due to my business engagements and a series of meetings that had come up. I did not prolong my conversation with Leena, but I did tell her that Lakshmi was aware of what her mother had done and that she had no interest in meeting her."

"Did Leena make a fuss?"

"Not much of a fuss, but I did hear her crying. As always, she was pretending to be the victim, blaming Prabhakar as the reason why she had never considered taking Lakshmi with her. Not that I would have allowed her to."

"One other thing," Dhananjay continued, "Leena's cousin, with whom I am still friends, attended their official marriage ceremony in London, the one where they go and sign in the register, etcetera. That cousin, his name is Dhruv, told me that Prabhakar openly denied ever being married before or having children from a prior marriage. That was one of the questions they have to answer in front of the state appointed person officiating the marriage. Of course, if he admitted to that, then he would have had to show them the divorce papers or some other proof of being previously married. Not only that, even socially, with friends and colleagues, whenever the topic of family and children came up, Prabhakar never mentioned his family in India."

Radha sat stunned, not moving, not breathing. Mamayya clenched his jaw, his fists balled up on the table. Dhananjay looked apologetically at Radha.

"I know this news would hurt your feelings Radha, but I had to let you know."

The small sliver of hope that she had entertained these three months, ever since the letter had arrived, the hope that perhaps Prabhakar would be able to assimilate with the family, Radha realized, was just a mirage. The very fact that Prabhakar could erase her existence, her children's existence spoke volumes. How could she have possibly thought that he would have changed or that he had any affection for her or his children? Again, she wondered if he even remembered his children's names. The divorce that Mamayya had spoken about now seemed a necessity and not symbolic anymore. Yes, she was ready to file for the divorce, she thought. But, what if Mamayya decided to forgive Prabhakar after coming face to face with him? A meeting with Prabhakar seemed more crucial than ever, because she wanted to gauge Mamayya's response. What if Mamayya was willing to accept him, back into the fold? After all a parent's propensity for forgiveness could be infinite. If Mamayya allowed Prabhakar back into the family, what would she do? Should she then choose to live separately, move into her own house leaving it to the children whether they wanted to move with her or stay back with their grandfather? Several minutes passed, Radha unaware that both Mamayya and Dhananjay were looking at her expectantly for a response. She came back to the present. A calmness had replaced the turmoil in her mind. She sat up, straightening her shoulders as though she had made up her mind about something. Both Mamayya and Dhananjay looked at her, waiting for her to speak.

"I know now what I am going to do, what I should do."

Before she could explain to both of them what she meant, Dhananjay exclaimed, "There he is," pointing in the direction of the large gates. He looked at his watch and said, "Our man is twenty minutes late." Outside the restaurant gates, they saw a man getting out of a car and talking to the driver. Perhaps, he was asking the driver to wait for him. Yes, it was Prabhakar alright, thought Radha.

He was wearing a white shirt and a blue suit and held a brief case.

Prabhakar stood hesitantly, looking around for a few brief moments and then started making his way towards the restaurant. He saw her and Dhananjay across the space separating them, across the chairs arranged in front of the dais, across the rock garden with its cactus plants and crotons and raised his hand, a half-hearted gesture in greeting. Radha wondered if he recognised Dhananjay, and chose not to acknowledge Prabhakar's greeting.

When Mamayya, who had been hidden by Dhananjay's broad frame, came around to stand in front of him, Prabhakar saw him and stood still. The music from the loudspeakers grew a few decibels and there was palpable excitement pulsating in the air around the restaurant. There were people filling up the rows in front of the dais. The Hanumans started dancing and singing.

Before Prabhakar could come any closer, he was surrounded by the Hanuman clones, their arms waving in rhythm to the *bhajan* playing on the loudspeaker. Their tails of varied shapes and hues were swinging in the light wind as they stamped in unison with the percussion. The ornaments they wore glinted in the brilliance of the setting sun as though the slanting rays of the sun were igniting flames of gold and glitter, red and green, the garlands they wore swayed with their bodies. Radha,

Dhananjay and Mamayya could see Prabhakar trying to push his way through the Hanumans. There was a short altercation as Prabhakar pushed one of the Hanumans onto a chair. Suddenly five or six of the Hanumans had surrounded Prabhakar and were lifting him up, crying loudly, "Jai Hanuman," and carrying him to the other side of the dais. Stupefied, Radha watched with Mamayya and Dhananjay as they lowered Prabhakar on to a chair and stripped the jacket and shirt off him. Then, one of the Hanuman clones splashed some blue paint on Prabhakar's torso. Radha saw Shanta talking to one of the Hanumans and wondered if this was all her doing or whether what was happening was unplanned and spontaneous. Could this be Shanta's revenge against Prabhakar for the incident years ago when he had rudely pushed her hand aside and called her a mad woman?

Radha looked up at Dhananjay for an answer and found him smiling, a look of satisfaction on his countenance, his arms across his chest. Was this Dhananjay's doing?

"You will be purified of all your sins," a Hanuman clone was announcing over the loudspeaker from the dais, "when you dress up as Lord Hanuman on this day. It is a rebirth."

Strangely, Radha felt no sympathy for Prabhakar. Yet, she was confused and even dismayed that her own innate decency, an armor she had worn through so many trials and tribulations, did not urge her to rush towards the entrance and the dais to rescue Prabhakar from his predicament. She recalled with painful clarity what Dhananjay had said a few minutes ago, about Prabhakar denying being married to her or having children with her, that he had visited India and never bothered to even call his father, if not her.

"What are they going to do to him?" she asked, her hand gesturing in the general direction of the group of Hanumans.

"Well, I don't know. He has got himself into quite a pickle, once again, hasn't he? He should not have provoked the Hanumans by pushing poor Shastry. As a group, the Hanumans can be very ferocious today." Dhananjay answered, scratching his chin. "Let us go and take a look. All this is totally unexpected."

So, Dhananjay was not responsible for this fiasco. Radha felt a sense of relief, relief quickly replaced by a feeling of guilt that she did not feel the compulsion to go and rescue Prabhakar. She had dreaded having a conversation with Prabakar by herself. Now, however, with Mamayya and Dhananjay flanking her, she was not afraid of facing him anymore. She would ask him all the questions that had been bottled up inside her all these years, she thought.

"I want to confront him," she said, "I want to face him boldly and without fear." Dhananjay nodded silently, as though he knew her thoughts and what was going on in her mind. Slowly, she walked towards the dais, towards the crowd of Hanuman clones. Mamayya and Dhananjay walked with her.

Shanta sprinted towards them, excitement writ large on her face. It was as if her normally high energy had doubled or even tripled this evening with all the festivities around. She greeted Dhananjay like an old friend and quickly bowed and touched Mamayya's feet. Mamayya put his hand on her head and joked, "Anjana Devi should not be touching my feet," whereupon Shanta laughed and said, "For you Mamayya, I am just Shanta, Akka's friend." Radha quickly pulled her aside and said, "Shanta, do you know that that man is Prabhakar, my husband and that I have come here to meet him?"

"Of course, Akka, I know everything. Dhananjay told me. Prabhakar hasn't lost his temper and arrogance, has he? He should not have pushed poor Shastry, making him nearly fall." Shastry was the head priest's young son who had decided to dress up as Hanuman for this festival. "He has really butted heads with the Hanumans. Even I cannot stop them. Don't worry, Akka, no harm will come to him. I will make sure of that. They will be parading with him for a short distance and taking him to the Hanuman Temple for the night-long worship. They will take care of him; they will even feed him and serve him tea. Of course, he will have to go without sleep, and he must deal with the inconvenience of washing away the paint after all the celebration, but that is a small punishment for all that he put you and your family through. Maybe, with Lord Hanuman's grace he will be purified. But please don't let him back into your lives." Having at once advised and assured Radha, Shanta rushed ahead, leading them to the centre of the crowd where Prabhakar was slouched on a chair, his briefcase lying by the side. They had finished painting his body a cobalt blue and his unpainted neck and face stood out in stark contrast. He had grown really fair living in the cold climates, Radha thought. She could tell that the fight in him had subsided, and he was not protesting or trying to get up from the chair. Approaching him, Radha looked at him, unafraid, with very little respect or sympathy and no affection at all. He had developed a double chin, his jawline not firm anymore, his nose, which she had thought perfect at one time, looked large and fleshy, his eyebrows had flecks of grey and there were dark circles beneath his eyes. His hairline had receded, his forehead wider, with furrows. His expression was sullen. Suddenly it was not Prabhakar's face that confronted her.

Instead she saw her little children walking to the school in the scorching sun, day after day, without the canopy of protection a father should have provided. Suddenly, she saw Atthayya, lying upon her cot, weak and emaciated, helpless. She saw Mamayya down in a heap sobbing uncontrollably beside the cot on which his wife had recently died. She saw, too, her two young children lying and nearly dying on cots in a local clinic, drips running through their tiny limbs, she saw the cut down on Sunanda's little ankle, the vein exposed as a white cord, the congealed blood at the incision site, her matted hair surrounding an angelic face on the pillow, dark circles around her closed eyes, she saw herself, Mamayya and Vasu taking turns in a week-long vigil by their side, immune to the pangs of hunger or thirst. She saw herself in a state of shock the first week after her husband abandoned them, herself spending interminable hours working in the nursery, digging, potting, carrying buckets of water, sacks of mud and packing compost in the hot weather, braving the elements for sustenance. She saw, too, a little girl, Lakshmi, Dhananjay's daughter, growing up without the love and guidance of a mother. She saw Dhananjay, a good decent, honest human being, struggling with the humiliation of a man deserted by his wife, the social ostracism, the challenge of being both a mother and a father to his little girl.

A white searing rage took over her. It was like nothing she had felt in all these years. Slowly, she advanced towards Prabhakar, all fear of him in her absolved, and stood before him. She did not feel inferior to him anymore. No, she was far superior to him because she had experienced poverty and insecurity, depression and sorrow and had conquered them. She had experienced what it was to be an abandoned wife and had overcome that and, in spite of all the travails, never forgot to be a loving mother, daughter-in-law, a source of strength and support for her children, a model parent for them, providing for their needs and education, a moral guide, a beacon that had lighted their paths to becoming what they were today: honest, decent and responsible human beings. Prabhakar looked up at her, guiltless, shameless, with anger and insolence in his eyes. Once, he had made her feel small and unworthy and had been openly disdainful of her. He had left them all without warning, without a backward glance, without any monetary help or support. Today, as she stood there, she was oblivious of the noise around her, the chanting and music emanating from the speakers. She wanted to say something or do something to show her disdain for him, her angst, her loathing. She wished she had a powerful eloquence and could summarise her antagonism to tell him calmly and coldly how unwelcome he was in their lives, but the torrent of words that rose to her lips was caught in the vortex of her emotions, making her realise that any words that she uttered in her rage would not be effective. Any book of chastisement or words of vitriol would be insufficient for what he had done to her, his parents and his children. Her eyes fell on the bucket of water in which the paintbrushes were immersed. The paints, red and blue oozing out of the brushes, were slowly mixing into a swirl of purple. She looked at Mamayya to see his reaction, whether he wanted to say anything to Prabhakar, whose gaze had now shifted from her to his father. Could this be the make or break moment, where the relationship between father and son could be repaired or forever forfeited? The expression on Mamayya's face was unfathomable. Would he be willing to forgive him or even rescue him from the predicament he was in?

With no warning whatsoever, Mamayya bent and picked up the brushes from the bucket. Taking a step forward, he threw them with all the force in his body on Prabhakar. The brushes made a short arc in the air across the distance that separated them, the red and blue paint spraying the air and the people around. Some of the paint fell on Mamayya's clothes, drops of red and blue scattered on Radha's saree and even on Dhananjay. Mamayya was oblivious to all that. A cheer went up from the Hanuman clones as the brushes landed on Prabhakar's head and face and slithered down his chest, finally resting on his belly. They had hit their mark, the red one first, splashing his forehead and nose, the blue bursting into colour on the rest of his face. As though this was not enough, Mamayya lifted the bucket of water and threw it at him, the purple colour running over Prabhakar's head and neck, creating large blotches on his face and chest.

"There, you have our answer, Prabhakar." Mamayya shouted, hoarsely with all the force in his lungs. "You have our answer." There was the glint of unshed tears in Mamayya's eyes.

A louder cheer went up again, this time from some of the onlookers and the Hanumans. Mamayya was getting ready to throw the empty bucket at Prabhakar too, but quite unexpectedly felt strong arms holding him back. He turned around to find Mukund, looking grim. "I think he got his answer, Thathayya," he said quietly, "let it go. You don't want to knock him unconscious."

Mamayya's anger dissipated as quickly as it had enveloped him, and the bucket clattered to the floor, the metallic sound jarring, grating, definitive, as though a heavy, impenetrable gate had closed on a chapter of their lives. At this point, all Radha was worried about was Mamayya and the toll this encounter was taking on him physically and emotionally. Mukund was very adroitly directing Mamayya away from the scene, and she was thankful for that. All this while, Dhananjay had stood very quiet, watching the drama unfold, but now, Radha saw him walking up to Prabhakar. Taking the broken plaque from his jacket, Dhananjay bent over Prabhakar to tuck it under his belt. It protruded over Prabhakar's potbelly like a sheath, a broken testament. "Here is the plaque with Leena's name on it, Prabhakar," Radha heard Dhananjay say. "Keep it as a memoir. Enjoy the rest of the evening. Have a happy *darshan* of Lord Hanuman."

Radha was about to turn and walk away when she heard Prabhakar say, "You planned all this, didn't you, Radha?" There was a quiet rage in his voice, and his look was spiteful. That he should even suspect her and hold her responsible for the turn of events showed Radha how little Prabhakar knew or even understood her. He did not seem to realise that he was responsible for raising the ire of the Hanumans with his arrogance and anger, for giving in to his belief of his own superiority. For the ten years they had shared, he had never once complimented or credited her for anything, but here he was crediting and holding her responsible for this unanticipated and even unique situation and his debasement. Why not accept the credit that was being thrown at her, Radha thought? The ludicrousness of the situation made her smile.

Instead, Radha looked him in the eyes and responded with a calm demeanor and a quiet but contemptuous tone, "No Prabhakar, you did this to yourself with your arrogance." With that she turned and walked away from Prabhakar. The anger that she had only moments ago experienced had fragmented, replaced by a feeling of wonderment at the unfolding strange conundrum of the evening. She realized that the throwing of the brushes and paint on Prabhakar by Mamayya had once and for all assured her about Mamayya's true feelings about his son. In a way, she had been absolved of the decision of allowing Prabhakar back into the family. Perhaps the cascade of events had been, in no small measure, the divine intervention of Lord Hanuman himself.

As she went back to the restaurant where Mamayya, Dhananjay, Vasu, Mukund and Sunanda were congregated, Radha was surprised at herself for being so calm and devoid of any hostile feelings towards Prabhakar.

"When did you arrive?" she asked her children.

"Just a few minutes ago, Amma," Sunanda answered, going up to her and embracing her.

"Do you want to go and see him, your father?" she asked Vasu and Sunanda.

"No," they answered in unison.

"Why don't we all eat, talk for a while and then go home?" Dhananjay suggested. They went back inside where the children, with the help of the waiters, joined two large tables and arranged the chairs around. Radha sat next to Mamayya, Dhananajay, opposite both of them. Moments later, Parvathi and Suresh joined them. Parvathi came and hugged Radha. As it turned out, she and Suresh were watching the events from the other side of the dais. Everyone, including Mamayya, had huge smiles on their faces as though they were all the recipients of an invaluable prize. It was only then that Radha realized how the impending return of Prabhakar into their lives had weighed so heavily on all of them.

"Are you all right, Mamayya? Will you be all right?" asked Radha. Mamayya laughed. "I have never felt better." Radha let out a huge sigh of relief.

"Did Prabhakar say anything to you?" Dhananjay asked.

"Nothing of consequence," Radha answered, smiling.

"Radha, you said something about making up your mind, that you had decided to do something. What was it?" Mamayya asked.

"I have decided to file for the divorce, for what it is worth, Mamayya." Mamayya smiled happily. "That is good news."

"What if Prabhakar refuses to sign the papers? He is capable of that, just to give me and us a hard time."

"Oh, no, he won't. I have his briefcase with his passport and all his documents." Dhananjay replied. "I snatched it when I bent over him to put the plaque under his belt. The threat of exposure of his past actions with regard to you all will work like magic and he will do what is asked of him. You see, a man like Prabhakar cannot afford to risk the bad publicity and what it might do to his business."

The food arrived, and everyone including Radha ate appreciatively. Kamalnath and Malathi were beaming with delight at the festivities out in the front and how well organized everything had turned out.

They heard Shanta's clarion voice speaking in elegant, literary Telugu, explaining the nuances of the *Sundara Kanda* over the loudspeaker.

Sundara *means beautiful and* Kanda *means chapter. It is that part of the Ramayanam which describes the great leap of Hanuman to Sri Lanka from the Indian subcontinent. The word Sundara has several interpretations, one being that Anjana Devi called her son*

*Hanuman "Sundara" because he was so beautiful. The whole book is very descriptive, not just of Hanuman himself, but all the wondrous and beautiful scenery he encounters as he is crossing to Lanka and the beauty of the island of Lanka itself; this is another reason for it being called Sundara, or beautiful chapter or book. Hanuman represents the inner strength that exists in all of us. This strength is often dormant and hidden, rising out of us and manifesting itself when life and its travails so demand, just as it happened with Lord Hanuman; the leap he made across the ocean represents our own leap of faith when we embark on an improbable task and when the goal seems so elusive. Lord Hanuman represents the strength and courage of a being who can defy the immutable laws of the Universe, one who can beat all odds for the betterment of himself and all mankind.*

The audience gathered in front of the dais and the diners in the restaurant sat spellbound as Shanta went on to enumerate further. She described the vast expanse and cerulean blue of the Indian Ocean, the hidden wonders at the depth of the ocean and the many challenges faced by Lord Hanuman as he flew towards Sri Lanka. There was thunderous applause at the conclusion of her speech. The music from the loudspeakers picked up again.

As they got up from the table, Radha could see the Hanumans dancing and singing, raising their hands, twisting their torsos, their forms, their tails, casting elongated shadows across the chairs and the dais. The Hanumans formed a formidable group as they advanced towards the steps leading to the temple. She knew that Prabhakar was lost somewhere in their midst. There were extra lights put up near the temple steps and small colourful bulbs on the Bougainville. They could hear the conches being blown in the temple and the peals of the temple bells resounding around the mountain and the restaurant. Radha wondered briefly if Prabhakar was in the complete attire of a Hanuman or whether they had left him to be a mere caricature with the thrown paint on his face and torso, with a broken plaque sticking out from under his belt.

As they drove home, talking all at once, laughing with relief and making plans for the future, Radha felt a lightness in her heart. This would be a most memorable evening for many reasons, for many years, she thought. The future loomed large and colourful in front of her. Yes, she breathed in the stale hot air with a hint of gasoline fumes, with a hint of the marigolds and jasmines; there was nothing wrong in being hopeful, even ambitious, about the future. She was not that rejected woman anymore. Life had showered her with so much wealth in the form of a wonderful, supportive father figure like Mamayya, her children and Tony, the support of Parvathi and Suresh, the friendship of the stalwart Dhananjay and a loyal friend like Shanta. Yes, they were all her guardian angels. And yes, she would always remember the grace of Lord Hanuman. As she leaned back against the seat, breathing a huge sigh of relief, she saw the lights of "Hotel Highway Very Most Famous" winking at her in the van's rear-view mirror.

*************************************************************